DATE DUE

The Monster of the Month Club Quartet:

Monster of the Month Club
Monsters in the Attic
Monsters in Cyberspace
Monsters and My One True Love

Monsters and My One True Love

Happy Holidays
To: Rilla Harmony Earth
Congratulations!
You have received a gift membership
to the *Monster of the Month Club*

January	February	March
Icicle	*Sweetie Pie*	*Shamrock*

April	May	June
Chelsea	*Burly*	*Summer*

July	August	September
Sparkler	*Butterscotch*	*Owl*

M.O.T.M. Club Rules:

1. A new monster selection arrives on the first day of every month.

2. The monsters come from different countries around the globe.

3. Instructions for the care and feeding of each monster are included in every box.

4. Good luck. . .

Monsters and My One True Love

Dian Curtis Regan

Illustrated by Melissa Sweet

Henry Holt and Company · New York

For my mother, Katherine French Curtis,
who I want to be just like when I grow up

Henry Holt and Company, Inc., *Publishers since 1866*
115 West 18th Street, New York, New York 10011

Henry Holt is a registered trademark of Henry Holt and Company, Inc.

Text copyright © 1998 by Dian Curtis Regan
Illustrations copyright © 1998 by Melissa Sweet. All rights reserved.
Published in Canada by Fitzhenry & Whiteside Ltd.,
195 Allstate Parkway, Markham, Ontario L3R 4T8.

Library of Congress Cataloging-in-Publication Data
Regan, Dian Curtis.
Monsters and my one true love / Dian Curtis Regan;
illustrated by Melissa Sweet. p.   cm.
Summary: In this final book in the
Monster of the Month Club quartet,
thirteen-year-old Rilla tries to maintain
secrecy regarding the monster toys
which arrive and come to life.
[1. Monsters—Fiction.   2. Toys—Fiction.]   I. Sweet, Melissa, ill.   II. Title.
PZ7.R25854Mnf   1988   [Fic]—dc21   97-50411

ISBN 0-8050-4676-3   First Edition—1998

Printed in the United States of America on acid-free paper. ∞
10   9   8   7   6   5   4   3   2   1

Contents

Monsters and My One True Love

Cast of Characters

January Selection

Name: Icicle   *Gender:* Male
Homeland: Botswana
Likes: Popsicles, frozen yogurt, iced lemonade
Keep in a cool, dry place.

February Selection

Name: Sweetie Pie   *Gender:* Female
Homeland: New Zealand
Likes: Pink bubble gum, flowers (pink only),
pink fruit punch
Doesn't like to be alone.

March Selection

Name: Shamrock   *Gender:* Male
Homeland: Ireland
Likes: Clover, raw potatoes, and green ginger bee
This one is a party monster.

April Selection

Name: Chelsea   *Gender:* Female
Homeland: Aruba
Likes: Kelp, salt water, tuna
Do not keep out of water too long.

May Selection

Name: Burly   *Gender:* Male
Homeland: Argentina
Likes: Baseball cards, Cracker Jacks, golf tees
Doesn't like to lose.

June Selection

Name: Summer   *Gender:* Female
Homeland: Portugal
Likes: Sunflower seeds, cola, worms
Needs plenty of room to exercise her wings.

July Selection

Name: Sparkler   *Gender:* Male
Homeland: Kowloon, Hong Kong
Likes: Hot dogs, chips, apple pie
Is fond of loud noises.

August Selection

Name: Butterscotch   *Gender:* Female
Homeland: Kathmandu, Nepal
Likes: Honey, granola, tofu
Shy. Needs lots of peace and quiet.

September Selection

Name: Owl   *Gender:* Male
Homeland: Rangoon, Burma
Likes: Poetry, numbers, literature
Never remove his glasses.

☆ 1 ☆

The Final Month

Rilla Harmony Earth pursed her lips to hold two tacks as she centered a sign on the bulletin board behind the Harmony House Bed and Breakfast registration desk.

Admiring her fancy artwork, she shoved the tacks into soft cork. Excitement made her hands tremble as she smoothed the sign:

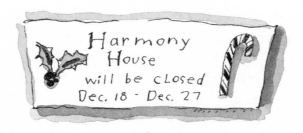

Harmony
House
will be closed
Dec. 18 - Dec. 27

Her excitement was sparked by a whole list of things.

1. Christmas was coming!

2. Aunt Poppy was getting married! (Reason the B & B would close temporarily.)

3. Her father would be here soon! (Even though Rilla was thirteen, she'd never met her father in person—only in cyberspace.)

4. Mr. Tamerow was on his way! (Her favorite B & B guest.)

5. Today was December first! (A new monster from the Monster of the Month Club waited in the mailbox.)

Rilla scooped a mailbag off the antique sideboard and raced out the double oak doors. Icy air, fogged with snowflakes, patted her cheeks and frizzed her hair as she ran across the slippery grass.

Why didn't I grab a jacket?

Shivering, she squeezed through the tight row of privacy pines bordering the yard. Were the shivers caused by winter's chill? The anticipation of meeting the newest monster? *Or* knowing that Joshua Banks (her one true love) might be waiting at the mailbox?

Joshua Banks was the only soul who knew about the monsters. He'd found out accidentally, but Rilla was glad to share her secret. Especially with *him*. Keeping monsters happy and fed was a big job for one person.

You've never had to deal with more than three monsters at a time, Rilla's inner voice reminded her.

True. Although today's arrival marked the twelfth monster to take up residence in her attic bedroom at Harmony House, only a few had come to life at the same time—thank heavens!

They were *supposed* to be stuffed "collectibles." Toys, in other words—not real, not alive. But the Legend of the Global Monsters *was* true:

Once, when stranger things than monsters roamed the earth, these tiny creatures shared nature with us, living in small colonies scattered throughout the world. Belief held that spotting a mini-monster in the wild meant good fortune would follow for a year.

Today, likenesses of the monsters have been created as cozy collectibles. Yet, legend warns, when stars line up in angled shapes like lightning, real global monsters tread the earth once more.

No one knew the legend was true—except Rilla and Joshua. The other home-schoolers who attended classes at the B & B didn't suspect a thing. Nor did Mr. Tamerow, who'd given her the one-year membership to the M.O.T.M. Club last Christmas.

Hurrying down Hollyhock Road to the neighborhood mailboxes, Rilla imagined announcing the monster secret to the home-schoolers for show-and-tell and pictured their reactions. . . .

Wally Pennington: "Is there a scientific equation to explain Project Monster of the Month?"

Marcia Ruiz: "If Rilla says it's true, then I believe her."

Andrew Hogan (in his Australian accent): "I'd believe *anything* Rilla told me."

Tina Welter: "Rilla is so weird. She's making up this stupid story just to get attention. Don't listen to her, Joshua Banks, do you hear me?"

Bah, humbug to Tina Welter.

"Hey, Earth!"

Rilla's head popped up. Only one person called her that. Ah, there was her one true love, loyally stationed by the Earth mailbox on his bike.

"Hi," she called, feeling self-conscious thanks to frizzy hair and her dumb lack of a jacket in freezing weather. "You're here!"

"Of course I'm here. It's Monster Day." Joshua grinned the double-dimpled grin she loved. "It's circled in red on my calendar."

Handing him the mailbag, Rilla's heart accelerated toward warp speed as she fished a key from her pocket. This monthly moment of anticipation had no equal in her life. She almost expected the entire universe to screech to a stop whenever she opened the mailbox and found a large parcel sporting foreign stamps.

Sque-e-e-eak went the hinges.

And there it was.

Catching her breath, Rilla reached in with both hands to claim the package. The shifting weight told her the box was occupied.

She clutched it to her chest. The shifting continued.

"It's alive!" she hissed.

Joshua leaned over the handlebars and cocked his head. "Listen!"

Rilla dropped to the curb. Wet snow soaked her jeans, but she didn't care. Curious, she held the box to one ear.

"Music?" Joshua asked.

Music?! Uh-oh. A live monster playing music will be a tough one to hide. She grimaced in answer.

A delivery truck turned onto Hollyhock Road, making Rilla jump to her feet. "Better get this one home. I mean, because it's alive and all." She brushed at the soaked spot on her bottom, feeling embarrassed.

Joshua turned his bike around. "I'm glad the home-schoolers are meeting at Harmony House today. When do you think I can sneak up to the attic to meet the monster?" He tapped a finger on the box.

Rilla wished the home-schoolers *weren't* meeting today. When she was the only student, there were more opportunities to check up on the monsters. "Might have to wait till after school."

Joshua curled his lip in disappointment.

Shoving the monster package into the bag with the rest of the mail, Rilla locked the box. "Gotta go. Sparrow gets mad at everything I do these days, so I can't be late for breakfast."

She bit her lip. *Don't say all that to Joshua.*

He scrinched one eye as if he understood. "See you in class." Pulling up the hood of his jacket, he shoved off on his bike.

Hugging the mailbag for warmth, Rilla ran back to Harmony House. The B & B was owned by her mom, Sparrow Harmony Earth (the former Donna Knox Pinowski), and her aunt, Poppy Harmony Earth (the former Sally Knox).

The Pinowski-to-Earth name change had become official when Rilla was only three. She tolerated her family's New Age philosophies while trying to appear normal—but it was hard. Other home-schoolers called their mothers "mom," but Sparrow insisted Rilla refer to her by name. It all had to do with her "mother as friend" theory.

Regardless, Sparrow had been HARD TO LIVE WITH the past few weeks. Blame it on the stress of planning Aunt Poppy's wedding, getting ready for the holidays, sprucing up the B & B for guests scheduled to arrive for the Christmas Eve wedding, *and* the fact that Rilla's father—Sparrow's former husband—was coming for a first-time visit. Ho, boy.

Rilla cleared her mind to focus on the problem at

hand. *How can I explain music coming from the mailbag? Maybe Sparrow won't be at the registration desk.*

Crossing her fingers for luck, Rilla slipped through the privacy pines, ran across the slushy grass, up the veranda steps, and tiptoed inside.

Sparrow was at the registration desk.

Rats.

Rilla tried to make herself invisible. Stepping softly across the parquet floor, she slid the mail onto the sideboard, hung up the bag, balanced the monster box discreetly on one hip—then made a mad dash for the stairs.

You can make it! You can make—

"Stop!" commanded Sparrow.

Rilla froze on the first landing. "What?" she blurted, then hoped she didn't sound snippy. Shifting the package, she kept it out of Sparrow's view.

Please don't ask me to open the box, she pleaded silently. With all the craziness at Harmony House this month, a live monster leaping from the package would certainly push Sparrow over the edge.

"Rill, it's eleven degrees and snowing. Why did you go outside without a coat? The *last* thing I need right now is a sick daughter."

Rilla relaxed her grip on the box. "Is that all?"

Sparrow peered up at her, as if looking for something else to gripe about.

Oops—don't give her more ammunition.

"No, that's not all, now that you mention it."

Way to go, Earth. . . .

"If you're not downstairs in ten minutes, you'll be late for breakfast, and that will be your third strike. No allowance this month."

"It's a new month," Rilla chirped. "I'm back to three strikes."

Sparrow peered at the calendar. "Oh, lord, you're right. How did December get here so fast?" She grumble-sighed. "Don't keep me waiting."

Rilla hurried upstairs, down the green-carpeted hall of family suites and herb-flower wallpaper, up another level to the blue-carpeted hall of single suites and moon-stars wallpaper, arriving at the narrow attic stairwell.

Unlocking the attic door with a key she wore on a silver chain around her neck, Rilla dashed inside and plopped the monster box onto her water bed. She grabbed scissors from her desk, but before she could begin to cut the mailing tape, she heard:

Snip, snip, snip . . .

Rilla watched the box pitch and wiggle, rock and tilt.

"Wow. Almost sounds as if whatever's inside is—"

Rr-r-r-i-i-i-i-i-p-p!

Rilla reared back in surprise. "It is!"

The December monster of the month was cutting its own way out!

☆ 2 ☆

The final Monster

Rilla scooted off the bed, eyes wide, listening to the monster rip, clip, and snip its way to freedom.

With a final slashing and slitting, a cat-size ball of red and green tumbled onto the quilt. Unfolding itself was a female, if long hair the color of Santa's red suit was a clue. Her clothes looked elfish: candy cane leggings, a pine green tunic, and a cap trimmed with golden bells that really tinkled.

Pointed ears, almost as long as her ski slope nose, held the jingly hat in place. Fuzzy white paws clutched tiny scissors, monster size.

Rilla watched the scissors disappear into a pocket and tried not to giggle out loud at the skinny creature, who looked like a Toyland refugee.

"Jingle bells, jingle bells . . ."

The music grew louder. Where was it coming from?

Rilla started to lift the monster to search for an

| 13 |

on-off switch, but a quick paw smacked her hand, making her reconsider.

The she-monster scrambled to her slippered feet and folded her tinsel-thin arms in a stance that said, "Do something!" even though the only words Rilla heard were *"laughing all the way."*

"Okay, okay." Rilla was used to monsters arriving hungry and grumpy after their long journey. "Let's see what's on your menu." Grabbing the box, Rilla shook it until the monthly selection card fluttered onto the quilt:

Monster of the Month Club
December Selection

Name: Bow   *Gender:* Female

Homeland: Baffin Island

Likes: Eggnog, pine needles, ribbon

The colder the weather, the happier the monster.

"Baffin Island?" Rilla mumbled. "Mmm. I'll bet it's near the North Pole since you're obviously a Christmas monster."

Bow didn't answer—not a surprise to Rilla. Only one of the monsters had talked (in English, that is). Owl. The September selection. At least all the others *understood* English even if they talked back in monster gibberish.

Rilla glanced at Owl. He was wedged between the computer and printer instead of nestled on her bed with the rest of the monsters and stuffed animals. She kept him there because that had been his favorite spot when he was "alive." Or "unstuffed." Or whatever the condition was called.

"Let's see . . . monster food." Rilla paused to think. "Pine needles. We haven't put up a Christmas tree yet, but we have plenty of evergreens in the yard. Ribbons are stored in the basement with the holiday decorations. Eggnog I can buy from Mr. Baca's One-Stop Shoppette."

Opening the bottom drawer of the dresser, Rilla stored Bow's "birth announcement" in a cookie tin with the other monthly selection cards. "I have to go downstairs now, but I'll be back later with food."

Bow glared at her. The music grew louder. *"UP ON THE HOUSETOP, REINDEER PAUSE . . ."*

Uh-oh. Maybe I'd better find monster food NOW.

Dragging a chair to the closet, Rilla climbed up to rummage through boxes on the shelf. In one she found a straggly yellow ribbon left over from a birthday present.

What luck! Hopping to the floor, she offered it to Bow.

The monster wrinkled her thin nose. Still, she snatched the ribbon and nibbled one end. Her teeth came to sharp points just like her ears.

"Bye for now," Rilla said. "Be quiet, take a nap, read, write a novel—whatever."

She waited for a reaction that didn't come. "Shouldn't a Christmas monster be, um, jolly?"

Bow glowered at her. Yellow ribbons must not taste very good.

Clank! Clank! Clank!

That was Sparrow, banging a spoon on the pipes that ran from the kitchen to the attic. One-minute warning.

Rilla grabbed her books from the desk and opened the door. The music worried her. "Can you please turn down your volume?"

"Jolly Old St. Nicholas" blared louder.

Big uh-oh. This could be a problem.

Afraid to say more, Rilla slipped out.

Mixed emotions swirled through her heart— dread at the problems another live monster brought into her life and sadness that December was the last month of the year. Bow was the final monster due to arrive in the Monster of the Month Club.

She loved all of them, every single one, no matter how grumpy, ornery, defiant, or rebellious. After all, it was the monsters who'd brought Joshua Banks and her together.

Rilla hurried down the back steps to the kitchen

(the servants' stairway in the old days). "Why not sign up for one more year of monsters?" she mumbled to herself.

The idea intrigued her. All she had to do was write to the M.O.T.M. Club home office in Oklahoma and renew her membership, right?

No! her conscience yelled back. *Why renew your membership? Look at how crazy the monsters have made your life.*

Rilla slowed her steps, realizing her inner voice was making a point worth listening to.

You already own twelve monsters. Isn't that enough for one person to watch over and care for?

But, she argued back. *I want to know more about the Monster of the Month Club. How many members are there? Are other kids hiding live monsters in their bedrooms, too?*

So write and ask about the M.O.T.M. Club. Just don't sign up for another year.

Mmm. Great idea. Pleased, Rilla skipped on down the stairs. *That's exactly what I'll do.*

☆ 3 ☆

Other B & B
Residents with Paws

Rilla made it to the kitchen with nary a second to spare.

Sparrow, wearing a flowered sweatshirt that read *I Wear the Plants in the Family,* perched on a stool at the counter, grading home-schooler papers. She glanced at the clock and nodded her approval at Rilla's arrival time. "But you still haven't fed the animals."

Rilla shifted her mind from monsters to cats and dogs. "I'll do it at break." Pausing to pour a glass of peach nectar, she added, "I *did* get the mail," to show her mother she *was* on the ball today.

Sparrow set the papers aside to put breakfast on the table (baked pears and an eggless omelette). "Rill, the cats are crying at the door. It's bad enough they have to live in the ice-cold barn; they shouldn't have to come begging for breakfast."

Guilt twinged Rilla's heart. Every time a monster

came to life, the cats and dog suffered from her lack of attention. "I'll run out and feed them right now," she said, wolfing down her food.

Muffled voices told her the home-schoolers were already arriving in the classroom. Dumping her dishes into the sink, she fetched a jug of water from the pantry.

"Wear my coat," Sparrow ordered.

Rilla grabbed her mother's coat off a hook. Yanking it on, she opened the door. Sure enough, Oreo, the mama cat, and her year-old kittens, Pepsi, Dorito, and Milk Dud, were whining at the door. Taco, the dog, wasn't in the yard.

Rilla fussed over the cats, begging their forgiveness, careful not to call them by name in front of her mother, who didn't believe in naming animals. Besides, health-nut Sparrow would have a fit if she heard the names her daughter had chosen.

Outside, the flighty snowflakes had organized and were falling in harmony. Turning up the collar of Sparrow's coat, Rilla absorbed calmness from the quiet snow piling up on the lawn and the roof of the greenhouse.

During the first frost of the season, she'd put the cats inside the greenhouse, thinking it'd be a warm, cozy spot for them to play and nap.

Bad idea. Aunt Poppy had caught the cats sampling greens, knocking over flowerpots, and using vegetable loam trays for a litter box. She was *real* unhappy with her niece that day.

The cats scampered across the yard ahead of her, sliding on slick stepping-stones. Inside the barn Rilla found Joshua Banks, playing chase with Taco around Aunt Poppy's Backyard Ride-a-Mower.

"Hello again," she exclaimed. "What are you doing?"

Joshua ruffled Taco's fur. "Kinda felt sorry for him, out here in the cold. I brought him a blanket." He motioned toward Taco's bed, made of old pillows and towels. "I fed him, too, but the water is frozen."

Rilla held up the jug she'd brought from the house.

He watched her pour cat crunchies into a row of dishes and fill the rest of the bowls with water.

"Well?"

She looked at his crinkled, questioning brow, knowing that he meant, *Tell me about the newest monster.*

"It's a girl," she said, feeling a sudden urge to hand out pink balloons.

"Seems right," Joshua told her, "since November was a boy."

Rilla pictured Cranberry, the November dragon-monster, relieved he was currently in his stuffed state. He'd almost set her quilt on fire with his flame breath.

Picking up Dorito, she sat on Aunt Poppy's weight-lifting bench and told Joshua all she knew about Bow.

He hung on every word, even though Taco was licking his face adoringly. "Do you think Bow will come and go like the last two?"

Come and go. That was a good way to describe what had been happening to Cranberry and Goblin, the October selection. "Don't know," Rilla answered. Having the monsters alive and real one minute, then silent and stuffed the next had certainly unnerved her.

Something weird was going on, but the explanation eluded her and Joshua. According to the Global legend, monster life was sparked by star patterns, yet heavenly bodies couldn't move *that* fast—could they?

"The telescope arrives today for our astronomy project," Rilla reminded him. "Maybe we can figure out if this has something to do with the comet and eclipse happening at the same time."

"Rill!"

Oops. "Better not keep Sparrow and Mrs. Welter waiting."

Rilla and Joshua bid a quick good-bye to the animals, then raced inside, stopping to hang their wet coats to dry. They hurried into the room behind the kitchen. In the old days it'd been the servants' living area but now served as a generous-size classroom.

New desks (compliments of Mr. Tamerow, sent last month from Finland) replaced the clunky tables and made the room look more like a real classroom.

Shelves along the perimeter housed ongoing projects (like the model of a medieval village made of cardboard and cloth), a class computer, and an aquarium, plus a variety of animals on loan from various sources. (The featured animal this month was a kea, a mountain parrot, on loan from a retired schoolteacher.)

Everyone settled in, gingerly sampling Sparrow's sesame semolina bagel bits. Mrs. Welter (Tina's mom) was fretting because the kea had chipped her nail polish. *Serves her right for teasing him,* Rilla thought.

Pausing by the world atlas, Rilla rose to her tiptoes and squinted at the very top—searching for Baffin Island.

Sparrow cleared her throat—which meant, "Take your seat."

Only Andrew asked Rilla what she was looking for. She didn't know if he was truly interested or merely wanted her to notice him.

"Just wondering where something was located." Feeling self-conscious, she took her seat, avoiding Andrew's gaze as well as Sparrow's.

Mrs. Welter stopped filing her nail and chuckled. "Well, we can't let a comment like that drop, can we, kids? Explain, Rilla?"

Tina groaned, shooting Rilla a look that said, "Thanks for the extra lesson."

"Um, I was looking for Baffin Island."

Tina mouthed the words *Baffin Island*? in a snarly sort of way.

"Near the North Pole," Wally said. "Way up top."

"I knew that," Rilla snipped. Every time the group played Trivial Pursuit, Wally memorized the answers. He had amazing retention.

"Marcia," Mrs. Welter said. "Call up Baffin Island on the encyclopedia, please."

Marcia swiveled her chair to face the computer, grabbed a CD-ROM, and booted it up.

"Two announcements while we wait," Mrs. Welter continued. "Our borrowed telescope will be delivered today so we can monitor the once-in-a-lifetime events happening in the skies over the next few weeks."

Everyone perked up. This sounded a lot more interesting than looking up stuff on the computer. Especially if one had a vested interest in relationships between star patterns and the way they affected stuffed toys who happened to be monsters.

Rilla glanced at Joshua. He wiggled his eyebrows at her in anticipation.

She glanced at Andrew. He winked.

Geez . . .

"The second announcement," Mrs. Welter

continued, "is from Andrew." She nodded at him to speak.

Andrew dipped his head in a sudden attack of self-consciousness. "Well," he began. "This is my last day of school. My father finished up at the university, so our family is returning to Australia."

Everyone began to fuss over Andrew.

Rilla watched him banter with the others while she absorbed the unexpected news. Wow. Andrew was leaving. He'd been her very first date and the first boy ever to hold her hand.

Mrs. Welter tapped her nail file on a desk to retrieve their attention.

Everyone hushed to listen to Marcia rattle off facts about Baffin Island.

Rilla knew there'd be no mention of monsters, so she didn't bother to listen. Instead she studied Andrew out of the corner of her eye.

Joshua Banks would *always* be her one true love. No doubt about it.

Still, in spite of how uncomfortable Andrew made her feel, Rilla had to admit that she hated to see him leave.

4

Goblin, Milk Dud, and the Giant Eye

To: President
   Global Gifts, Inc.

From: Rilla Harmony Earth

Dear Mr./Ms. President,
   I am writing for information about the Monster of the Month Club. Please send <u>complete details</u>. Thank you.

Rilla underlined the words *complete details* so they'd know she wanted *all* the facts about the club and the monsters. After waiting for the letter to ooze through the printer, she signed her name, imitating Sparrow's slanted handwriting so the prez wouldn't guess she was a kid:

Rilla Harmony Earth

She addressed the envelope to the M.O.T.M. Club home office in Oklahoma City and pasted on a stamp. Then she drank Bow's mug of eggnog because the December monster wouldn't be needing it now.

Rilla sighed. Having the monsters "come and go," as Joshua called it, made her sad. She'd barely had a chance to get to know Bow, yet there she sat on top of the dresser, still and silent. No more holiday music.

Matter of fact, it was Goblin, the October selection, who was alive and well this afternoon, acting her strange, mysterious self.

"Gob, are you hungry?"

One eye, shadowed by the brim of a slouch hat, peeked around the bedpost. The monster's fangs glimmered in the afternoon light slanting through the attic windows. Rilla'd had nightmares about those fangs ever since Goblin had arrived.

Opening her dresser drawer, she pulled out a bag of candy corn.

Goblin scuttled around the bed to the dresser, then cupped both paws while Rilla sprinkled in candy. The monster wolfed it down, then cupped her paws again.

The look in Gob's dark eyes was *not* one of pleading—like most of the monsters at feeding time. It was more like, "Food. Now. Or else." It was the "or else" part that made Rilla keep plenty of October monster food on hand.

That and the cryptic "Beware" warning on Gob's card:

Monster of the Month Club
October Selection
Name: Goblin   *Gender:* Female
Homeland: Transylvania
Likes: Candy corn, hot cocoa, spiders
Beware . . .

So far, Rilla hadn't catered to Goblin's taste for spiders. Yuck!

She watched the monster devour a third pawful of candy corn. Gob's resemblance to a werewolf did *not* go unnoticed, even though she wore a trench coat. Once Rilla tried to smooth her raggedy gray fur with Taco's wire brush, but it seemed to grow longer and more tangly.

Goblin's eyes bothered Rilla the most. Even more than the fangs. Dark and aloof, they watched her every move, as if . . . as if what?

Monsters were too smart to bite the hand that fed them. Weren't they?

Rilla glanced at the clock. Time to get downstairs. The home-schoolers had taken a long lunch break while the telescope was being set up in the backyard.

Bundling up in her warmest jacket, she hurried outside. "Whoa," she mumbled when she saw the telescope. It was much larger than she'd expected. Mrs. Welter had asked the university to send one powerful enough to view the stars and the comet, soon to debut in the northern sky.

The scope looked like a fat zoom lens on a camera—only big enough for a giant. It was positioned on a sturdy tripod with wheels, on the cement walk next to the greenhouse.

Rilla waited her turn for a peek through the lens. Sparrow was letting everyone practice by demonstrating how to bring the neighbors' naked trees into focus.

Rilla peered into the eyepiece. With one turn of a knob, housetops blocks away jumped into her face, magnified a zillion times.

"Nifty," Rilla exclaimed. "I can see Mr. Tafoya's frozen towels hanging on his clothesline."

Everyone chuckled except Tina, who was busy cooing to Milk Dud. The cat peeked out from his snuggly place inside her jacket. Tina always snatched up Milk Dud whenever she came to Harmony House.

It annoyed Rilla.

"Okay, we've all had a chance to play with the giant eye," Mrs. Welter said. "Obviously the sky has to be dark before we can see what's going on up there, so here is our schedule for evening classes."

She paused while Sparrow handed out a blue sheet noting dates and times. "At the bottom is a permission slip for your parents to sign, letting us know it's okay for you to be here for night viewing."

Night viewing? Midnight rendezvous beneath the stars?

Rilla glanced at Joshua, but he was concentrating on the schedule. *This could be fun.*

"It will be cold out here while we do our viewing," Mrs. Welter added. "Dress for the occasion. Wouldn't want anyone getting sick for Christmas."

On cue Milk Dud sneezed, making everyone laugh.

"That's it for today," Sparrow said. Opening the greenhouse door, she helped Mrs. Welter roll the telescope inside for safekeeping. "Everybody meet in the kitchen. Hot cocoa awaits."

The home-schoolers dashed for warmth—except Tina. She clung to Milk Dud, whispering to him.

Rilla's feeling of maternal possessiveness made her stay behind. "He can't come inside."

"I know," Tina shot back. "And I think it's a crime."

"Huh?"

"At *my* house he'd be an indoor cat. He'd never have to face another cold winter. He'd have his own pillow by the fire, and he wouldn't have to fight others for food."

"He doesn't have to fight. . . ." Rilla's voice trailed off. Actually the cats *did* scramble for a place at the food bowls. "He's mine," she snipped, cringing at the whine in her voice. She sounded like a two-year-old.

"You have other cats," Tina reasoned. "I don't."

"So get one."

"I want Milk Dud."

You want Milk Dud because he belongs to me, Rilla added to herself, wishing Sparrow would stop insisting the cats stay outside to appease B & B guests with allergies.

Tina sniffed. "But Milky knows me. He talks to me. He cries when I put him down." Now Tina sounded whiny. "See?" she said, demonstrating.

Milk Dud gave a pitiful meow, lifted his front paw, and shook off the snow.

"He'd cry if *anyone* moved him from a warm coat to a snowdrift," Rilla countered.

"Girls!" Mrs. Welter knocked on the storm door, waving them inside.

Tina scooped Milk Dud back into her arms, kissed him on the nose, then carried him to the barn so his paws wouldn't get any wetter.

Rilla trudged toward the house. That was the longest conversation she'd ever had with Tina without suffering one insult aimed at the Earth family.

Scooping up a handful of snow, Rilla pitched it toward a hackberry tree in an attempt to show Tina how disgusted she felt.

Unfortunately Tina's sincerity—plus Milk Dud's pathetic mewing—made Rilla feel more disgusted with herself.

Go figure.

5

Aunt Poppy's Fitting

"Turn."

Aunt Poppy obeyed her big sister's command, pivoting in her stocking feet on the ottoman in Sparrow's bedroom.

"Wow," Rilla exclaimed, stepping into the tiny room tucked behind the parlor. Aunt Poppy's wedding dress was almost finished. Sparrow still planned to sew tiny pearls onto the bodice after she finished adding a layer of lace over the silk skirt.

Sparrow motioned for Rilla to shut the door, then stuck a half dozen pins into her mouth and waited for the bride-to-be to turn again.

Aunt Poppy grinned in greeting. She'd been grinning a lot lately. Rilla figured it was because she was happy and in love.

Poised on the ottoman in the warm lamplight, she looked positively radiant. Didn't even resemble a former-hippie-turned-innkeeper, but a princess in a fairy-tale gown. Her hair was twisted up off her neck and knotted with a holiday scrunchie. The formfitting dress proved that Aunt Poppy's weight-lifting sessions in the barn were time well spent.

The wedding silk had been ordered from a tailor in Japan, recommended by Mr. Tamerow. Sparrow had requested pale gold for two reasons—it was a Christmas color, and it was her little sister's fifth trip to the altar.

But Aunt Poppy had insisted on reordering *white* silk. After all, it was the groom-to-be, José's, *first* trip down the aisle. (He was a musician from Montana who'd made Harmony House his home away from home.)

Rilla had thought the whole argument ridiculous. Brides should wear whatever they wanted. When the silk arrived, it wasn't white after all but off-white. Rilla suspected it was one of Sparrow's "on-purpose accidents." A big sister–little sister jab.

"Dint live," Sparrow said.

"Huh?"

Sparrow removed pins from her mouth. "Don't leave. You're next."

Rilla nodded. Her bridesmaid dress, draped over the ironing board, was made of the holiday gold originally intended for the bride. The satiny material sparkled in the light.

She loved the dress—poofy arms, poofy skirt.

What she didn't love was the low-cut neckline. No big deal, really, but she hated the way the bodice fit her the same way it fit the hanger. A bit of a bosom would be nice, but Rilla didn't count on one appearing within the next few weeks. *Sigh.*

Wouldn't it be nice if Joshua could see her all dolled up with her hair French braided the way Aunt Poppy promised to fix it? Maybe she would stumble into her one true love in the barn on the wedding day.

Right, Earth, you'll be dressed in your gown, feeding the cats, and Joshua won't have anything better to do on Christmas Eve than hang out in the barn with Taco.

Rilla laughed to herself. Even better was the thought that her father would see her in this lah-de-dah dress. And see how grown up she was. Rilla shivered. Thinking about him made her nervous. In a matter of weeks, he would be right here at Harmony House. Yikes.

R-r-r-r-i-i-i-i-i-ng!

"Should I get it?" Rilla offered.

"No," Aunt Poppy said. "José is stationed at the registration desk."

Rilla acted appalled. "You mean, he just arrived and you've already put him to work?"

Aunt Poppy flung a thimble at her. "Well, if he's going to be an Earth, he'd better learn the B & B business."

"Oh, please tell me he's not changing his name to Earth."

Rilla hated the way the Earth sisters imposed their philosophies on people around them—like expecting the home-schoolers to snack on sesame semolina bagel bits.

"No, he'll remain a Pacheco and still travel to his gigs, but he'll play here most of the time."

"Here? You mean, José will play music for the guests?"

Her aunt nodded vigorously, emulating Rilla's enthusiasm.

"Quit wiggling," Sparrow ordered.

Aunt Poppy made a face at her big sister when she wasn't looking.

Rilla giggled. It was brave of her, under the circumstances.

While waiting for her fitting, Rilla toured Sparrow's bedroom. Decorations were sparse, not overdone like Aunt Poppy's room. A colorful quilt cozied up the bed, and a hand-braided rug covered the floor. The only pictures on the wall were of Rilla.

She stopped to groan at each one:

Rilla—first day of school.

Rilla—two front teeth missing.

Rilla—sitting on Nancy, the goat, who used to "mow" the lawn before neighbors' complaints sent the goat off to a farm east of town.

Picking up a music box, she wound it. Strains of "Give Peace a Chance" drifted from the rosewood box, adding to her melancholy mood.

After dinner she'd taken a mug of hot cocoa to Goblin, only to find her beneath the rocker, not moving, not a spark of life shining in those dark, creepy eyes.

Rilla had drunk the cocoa, setting the mug next to Bow's empty cup of eggnog she'd polished off earlier.

Worst of all, she'd had to uninvite Joshua to the attic since there were no new monsters to meet.

This was unsettling—like the quiet before an earthquake when birds become still and animals shiver and hide. They know something big is about to happen.

That's how this "coming and going" business made Rilla feel—like she was waiting for a page to turn or the next scene in a play to begin.

"Hey," came José's voice from the hallway as he tapped on the door.

"Stop!" Aunt Poppy shrieked. "Don't come in!" Hopping off the ottoman, she raced to the bathroom, muttering, "He's not supposed to see me in my wedding dress."

Sparrow winced as lace snagged on the bedpost. "What is it, José?"

He peeked into the room, waving at Rilla. "The

phone call was from Abe. He's at the airport. Soon as they round up bags and a cab, he'll be on his way."

"Mr. Tamerow is here!" Rilla yelped. Dear Mr. Tamerow. The giver of the monster gift. The B & B guest she adored. The one who came too infrequently and departed too soon. He was here at last, but . . .

Reality filtered into Rilla's memory. On Mr. T.'s last trip—to Finland—he'd gotten married. Not only that, but his bride, Minna, a widow, had kids. Twins! Two four-year-olds.

Never again would Rilla have Mr. Tamerow all to herself. Now she had to share him with Flopsy and Mopsy—or whatever the heck their names were. She'd forgotten.

You have not forgotten, her inner voice scolded. *Aleksis and Elias. The names were burned into your memory the minute you got the news.*

Oh, hush up! she whisper-hissed at her inner voice.

She didn't want to know their names, and she *certainly* didn't want them coming to Harmony House with *her* Mr. Tamerow.

Hummmph.

☆ 6 ☆

Bunking with Monsters

"Oh, lord," Sparrow exclaimed. "I didn't expect Abe to arrive for the holidays until next week. Thanks, José." She waved him out the door before Rilla could ask any questions.

"Get dressed!" Sparrow hollered to Aunt Poppy as she ripped off her pincushion bracelet and pitched it into her sewing basket. "We've got to find beds for everybody."

"Is José gone?" came a muffled voice from the bathroom.

"Yes," Rilla called.

"We'll do your fitting later," Sparrow told her. "Hang up your dress for now."

Rilla followed orders, muttering, "Maybe by later I'll have a bosom."

"Don't disappear," Sparrow added. "I may need your help."

Rilla wandered toward the foyer, resisting the urge to pack up and move into the barn with Taco and the cats so she wouldn't have to witness Mr. Tamerow and his kids together.

"Hey," said José, perched on a stool behind the registration desk. His earring glimmered in the lamplight. "Come help me polish room keys. They're getting tarnished." He held one up to the light.

Rilla wasn't in a joking mood. "I'll go buy silver polish," she deadpanned. "On Baffin Island." She'd do anything not to be here when the Tamerow family arrived.

José was quiet for a moment, humming a song.

Rilla wondered if he was making up a new melody in his head.

"Ohhhhhhh, I get it," he began. "I know what's bugging you."

Rilla returned his stare. "No, you don't." She tried to sound sarcastic, but she liked José too much to be nasty.

He cowered playfully at her abrupt answer. "Give me three guesses?"

She shrugged, absently thumbing through a stack of Harmony House Christmas cards. "Okay. Go."

José swiveled the desk lamp so the light shone on Rilla's face as though he were interrogating her. "The guy with the accent hasn't asked you out again."

Her face warmed—but not from the heat of the lamp. How did José know about Andrew? Oh, yeah, he'd been visiting the day she'd gone on her movie date. "That has nothing to do with it. Besides, he moved away."

Rilla rearranged pencils in Sparrow's *Every Day Is Earth Day* mug. "And your second guess?"

José tapped a hand on his cheek, thinking. "You're jealous that your aunt is getting married instead of you."

She mustered her best disgusted expression. "Get real."

He emulated her expression. "Third and final guess?"

"Go."

"You're unhappy that Abe got married."

Rilla dropped a handful of pencils. *How could he know that?*

"Aha." José snapped his fingers. "You're upset because Abe has a made-to-order family and you worry about being pushed out of his life."

She was shocked by how vividly he could read her heart. "Okay, Dr. Pacheco, who told you?"

"Nobody. I'm an artist. I observe people for a living. You were in a goofy mood at dinner, and now—"

"Only because you hid your beet slivers beneath a spinach leaf so Sparrow wouldn't notice you weren't eating them."

He pretended to be stunned. "Spying on me? Ah, you must be an artist, too. I *hate* beets." He pinched her cheek. "As I was saying, you shifted from goofy to end-of-the-world way too fast—even for a teenager."

Rilla sighed, hating to admit he was right. "So?"

"Look at it this way. Harmony House is more fun when guests with kids come to stay. They race up and down the green hallway. Leave fingerprints on windows. Track mud on the carpet."

Rilla chuckled at his list of all the things Aunt Poppy hated since she had to clean up after guests' children. "Okay. I apologize for being crabby."

Inside, she didn't feel any different. Perhaps she should mosey up to the attic instead of standing around waiting for the awful moment when the Tamerows arrived.

But before she could head for the stairs, Sparrow and Aunt Poppy came flying around the corner. José hopped out of the way so the sisters could study the guest register.

Aunt Poppy, dressed in faded jean overalls and a baggy flannel shirt, waist-length hair hanging limp, had transformed from a princess back into . . . well, an aunt. The fairy-tale glow was gone.

"No family suites are open." Sparrow groaned. "I was afraid of that."

Aunt Poppy pointed at the ledger. "Here's a single suite. B-2. The small one beneath the attic."

"There's no room in B-2 for the kids," Sparrow told her.

"I'll give up my room," offered José.

"But we can't let the kids stay alone. They're too young. What if they wake up in the middle of the night and don't know where they are?"

"Then I'll baby-sit the little guy," José said. "He can have the bed, and I'll set up the futon and sleep on the floor."

Aunt Poppy's face got all misty and tender. "Oh, that's so sweet of you. And I'll bet the girl can bunk with Rilla."

Rilla's breath *swooshed* from her body. The grandfather clock stopped ticking. The lights dimmed. The earth came to a standstill.

All three grown-ups stared at her.

"Sound okay, Rill?" Sparrow asked.

"I—I . . ." It was hard to talk with no breath left in one's body.

One of the twins in my attic? All night? What if the monsters come to life? No, no, no, no, no. This will never work.

"Be a sport, kid," Aunt Poppy said. "The girl is too old to wet the bed, and she's jet-lagged from the long flight. She'll probably sleep like a brick."

Rilla wasn't worried about Flopsy. She worried about the monsters. Leaping to life in the middle of the night. Scaring little girls. Little girls who'd scream and tell.

Sounded like a horror novel, which is what this might turn into.

Sparrow elbowed her impatiently. "Rill, it's only for one night. A family suite will open up tomorrow after checkout. Then we can move all the Tamerows into one room."

Rilla *really* wanted to get the earth rotating again. She nodded, unsure of her voice.

The light brightened. The grandfather clock began to tick.

But she still couldn't breathe. . . .

☆ 7 ☆

Now There Are Four

"I'll—I'll run upstairs and see if my room is, um, clean."

Rilla's voice was so breathy, she hardly recognized it. The disappointment in her mom's eyes told her she'd lost ground in her ongoing battle to convince Sparrow that she was responsible.

Rilla wanted to say, "I don't *mind* sharing my room. Honest." It wasn't the sharing part at all. What was she supposed to do about the monsters? Hope the little girl didn't notice strange creatures roaming the attic?

Yeah, right.

Dashing upstairs, Rilla ignored the "Do not run in the hallways or you'll disturb guests" rule. This was an emergency!

Inside the attic, peace and quiet reigned. Could she be so lucky?

Then muffled scritch-scratchings drew her to the

tiny bathroom. The open cabinet door tipped her off on who had sprung to life.

Cranberry, the November monster.

During his "live" moments, he'd built a nest in the towel cabinet. Mainly for the purpose of hoarding things. Rilla's things.

She cleared her throat to warn him of her approach. Once, she'd startled him and was rewarded with singed eyebrows from his fiery breath.

Stepping loudly across the tile, Rilla gingerly flicked the cabinet door open. Cranberry pawed rapidly at the towels, as if attempting to hide something.

Rilla sat cross-legged on a round rug. The monster's fur matched his name and was sewn in wavy layers, like fuzzy scales. His face was the most animal-like of all the monsters, dominated by a long, narrow snout.

A row of furry ridges cascaded down the back of his head, disappearing beneath a nubby wool sweater. Cutouts allowed two tiny wings to emerge.

Rilla figured the wings were ornamental. Once Joshua tried to teach Cran how to fly by tossing him into the air, then flapping his arms to show the monster how to flap his wings.

Cran loved it, immediately bonding with Joshua, even though the poor thing kept crash landing on the water bed.

The flying lesson had left Rilla on the floor in

hysterics. She figured Cranberry thought Joshua was his mother.

"Hi, Cran," Rilla cooed, hesitant to move too fast. "What are you hoarding today?" Lifting a corner of a washcloth, she found a half-eaten yellow ribbon.

"You stole Bow's dinner!"

His smoldering look read, "If I find it, it's mine."

No way was she going to get the ribbon away from him. "Well, Joshua will be pleased to know you're back with us."

Cranberry licked his snout, much like Taco did. Curling into a ball, he hung his front paws over the edge of the towels, batting at Rilla each time she tried to peek at today's treasures.

Suddenly Rilla remembered why she was there.

Better subdue the monster with food so he'll nap and be quiet.

Digging through the dresser, she found a stash of acorns. Then she fished Cran's birth announcement from the cookie tin to remind her what else he liked to munch:

Monster of the Month Club
November Selection
Name: Cranberry   *Gender:* Male
Homeland: China
Likes: Acorns, pumpkin seeds, apple cider
Keep away from matches.

Rilla scoffed at the warning. Cran didn't need matches. His smoky breath sparked flame far too easily for her comfort.

Back in the bathroom, she lined up a row of acorns inside the cabinet. "Please stay here and be quiet," she pleaded.

Two seconds after closing the door, she heard Cranberry crunching the acorns.

Rilla checked on Bow and Goblin. Both fast asleep. Semi-permanently, no doubt.

Maybe this will work. If only Cran will stay quiet. She crossed her fingers as she trudged downstairs.

Commotion below told her Mr. Tamerow had arrived. Once an occasion for joy, Rilla now felt dread. "Tamerow" no longer meant Mr. T.

"Now there are four," she muttered. "Three too many."

She stopped on the first-floor landing to watch the scene below.

"Rilly!"

Mr. T. grinned up at her. In his arms was a sleeping child with a mass of red curls.

Before Rilla could return his greeting, Mr. Tamerow's attention switched to a small boy yanking on his overcoat.

"Now!" the boy demanded.

Aunt Poppy leaped to the rescue, taking the child's hand and leading him to the hall bathroom.

Sparrow scooped the sleeping twin from Mr. T.'s arms and disappeared into the parlor to deposit her on the sofa.

Introductions followed, with much fussing over Minna, the new Mrs. Tamerow.

Rilla sat on a step to watch. Minna looked kind. She was tiny and petite. Bushy red hair was tied back with a green velvet ribbon.

Coats and gloves and hats came off. José rushed about collecting them and stacking bags to carry upstairs.

Minna's gaze shifted to Rilla. Her face brightened. "You must be the one I've heard so much about."

Embarrassed, Rilla stood, sidestepping José as he carried luggage upstairs.

Minna climbed the steps and held out both hands. "I'm pleased to meet you at last."

Rilla had been so prepared not to like the new Mrs. Tamerow that she didn't know how to respond, other than to squeeze Minna's hands in return and hope she spoke again because her soft Finnish accent was very appealing.

Mr. T. bounded up the steps and scooped Rilla into a hug.

Of course Mr. Tamerow would marry someone who was kind and gentle like him. This shouldn't surprise her.

Rilla peeked over his shoulder and returned Minna's smile. In spite of everything she'd been feeling, she couldn't help but like Mr. T.'s bride.

It was those redheaded twins she wasn't too sure about.

☆ 8 ☆

A Sleep Over with Aunt Rilly

Sparrow explained the temporary sleeping arrangements, then disappeared to prepare coffee and scones.

Aunt Poppy led the newlyweds to their suite. Rilla helped carry the futon to José's room, then rounded up sheets, blankets, and pillows while José and Aunt Poppy put Elias to bed.

Mr. Tamerow fetched the sleeping twin from the parlor and carried her to the attic. Rilla pleaded silently with Cranberry every step of the way.

Please stay in your cabinet. Don't come out to see what's going on.

When they hit the attic stairwell, she added: *Please don't let any of the other monsters be alive. Not for the next ten minutes.*

Rilla wasn't sure to whom she was making this urgent request, yet she hoped whoever was in charge of star patterns obliged her.

The attic was dark and quiet. Instead of clicking

on the overhead light, Rilla turned on the lamp next to the bed for a softer glow. She whisked her stuffed animals off the pillow and piled them in the rocker.

Among the four lions, bear, rabbit, walrus, rhino, etc., were Icicle, Sweetie Pie, and Shamrock (the January, February, and March monsters).

Lined up on the bookshelf were Burly, Summer, Sparkler, and Butterscotch (May, June, July, and August). Owl (September) was in his spot between the computer and printer. And Chelsea (April) was on a shelf over the tub in the bathroom. She was a mermaid-monster, so the tub had been her home when she was "alive."

Goblin was still beneath the rocker, where she liked to hang out. Bow was on top of the dresser. As the newest monster, she was the one most likely to spring to life. Rilla had even laid out a red ribbon (snitched from the Christmas gift wrapping box) just in case Bow "woke up hungry."

Rilla yanked back the quilt so Mr. T. could slip his new daughter beneath the covers. Her pink sweatsuit would have to double for pajamas.

"Her name is Aleksis," Mr. Tamerow whispered. "Usually she's not this quiet." He chuckled at his own joke.

A scratching sound echoed from the bathroom. Mr. T. glanced in that direction—as if he expected to see someone enter the room.

Hush, Cran!

Mr. Tamerow started to tuck the quilt around the sleeping child.

Rilla stopped him. "You forgot to take off her shoes."

"Blame it on jet lag," he said, removing them. "Thanks."

Faint music began to play. "*Let it snow, let it snow, let it snow. . . .*"

Mr. T. peered around the room. "Did you turn on a radio?"

Oh, yikes.

Rilla glanced at Bow. The monster's eyes followed her movements.

Please don't move. Don't get up. Don't—

The music grew louder.

"My radio alarm must be set for the wrong time," Rilla explained in a suddenly shaky voice. "I can fix it."

Rilla lunged for the door, hoping Mr. T. would follow. But he hunched over the tiny lump in the bed, fussing with the blankets. "She likes to hear a story before she falls asleep."

"I'll tell her one," Rilla blurted. "I mean—if she wakes up."

"She might be frightened if she doesn't know where she is," he added in a thoughtful tone.

"I'll . . . I'll . . ." Rilla paused, not sure what to do in that situation.

"But I've told her so much about you," he continued, "and she's been really excited about coming here and meeting you. I'm sure she'll be tickled to wake up and find herself having a sleep over with Aunt Rilly."

Aunt Rilly?

"Better get downstairs," Rilla urged. "Coffee and scones await."

Mr. T. tucked in the quilt, tiptoed halfway across the room, then paused. "Could you shut off that music so it doesn't wake her? Seems to be getting louder."

Oh, boy. Rilla had *no* idea how to shut off the music.

Behind Mr. T.'s back, Bow stood on her spindly candy cane legs and stretched, as if waking from a nap. In the dim light, she looked so bizarre—like a Keebler elf, escaped from a bag of cookies.

"Um, the radio's pretty complicated. I may have to take it apart, and, well, I *really* need to get downstairs first to see if Sparrow needs me. She's been so hard to live with lately. I think it's because my dad is coming for Christmas, and—"

"Oh, your *father!*" Mr. Tamerow exclaimed. "Poppy told me you found him through the Internet. How fabulous. I can't wait to meet him."

Yes! Change the subject. Get Mr. T. out of here!

"When do you expect him to arrive?"

Talking fast, Rilla grabbed Mr. T.'s sleeve and drew him out the door, filling him in on the details about her father. She wasn't worried about leaving Aleksis alone for a few minutes. How would Bow even notice a tiny lump in the bed, fast asleep?

On the way downstairs, she thought about the times she'd tried to tell Mr. Tamerow the truth about the monsters. How the legend was more than a legend. How the monsters were real, not cozy collectibles the way the Monster of the Month Club said they were.

Yet now that she'd had a perfect opportunity to prove it to him, she'd chosen not to. Why?

Rilla puzzled over the reason. Sharing the secret with Mr. T. (alone) was one thing, but now he was part of a family. Could she trust him to keep her secret any more than she could trust Sparrow to let the monsters remain with her in the attic?

You're still angry with him for acquiring a family without your permission.

He doesn't need my permission. He's a grown-up.

Aha. A grown-up. That's the real reason you'll never tell him the truth about the monsters. . . .

Downstairs, Sparrow poured coffee and tea while José fetched extra chairs for the kitchen table.

"Here they are," Aunt Poppy exclaimed. "Sit down, Abe, and tell us how you and Minna met. We want to hear the entire story."

"Yes, tell us," Sparrow urged, handing a stack of napkins to Rilla.

Aunt Poppy set honey and soy milk on the table, then lifted raisin scones from the oven. The aroma of nutmeg and spiced tea gave a Christmassy feel to the kitchen.

Rilla quickly slapped a napkin next to each plate. Her urgency to return to the attic was stronger than her desire to eat a warm scone, no matter how heavenly they smelled.

Sparrow was fussing over Minna's wedding ring. Rilla yanked on her mother's apron. "Do you need me?" she whispered.

"No, but stay, Rill. We haven't seen Abe for months. Have a seat."

Rilla tried to look apologetic. "I really think I should get back upstairs. If Aleksis wakes up, I'll be there."

"Oh, how sweet," gushed Minna. Turning to her new husband, she added, "Rilla is just as dear as you told me."

Guilt heated Rilla's neck. So her motives weren't pure. She wanted to get back to the attic to check on Bow and Cranberry, too.

Minna touched her arm. "If you need us or if Alek bothers you, please come knock on our door."

Sparrow acted so pleased at the way Minna had

praised her incredibly responsible daughter, Rilla's guilt level rose twelve notches.

Minna glanced at her watch. "Let's see. It's nine P.M. here, so it would be . . ." Pausing, she counted on her fingers. "Four o'clock in the morning in Helsinki. Alek might be up in a few hours because of the time change. I hope she doesn't wake you at an unearthly hour."

"Not a problem," Rilla said, figuring she'd have to stand guard all night anyway for Operation: Keep Twins and Monsters Apart.

"Thanks, love," Minna said.

Rilla dashed upstairs. Earlier she'd hoped the monsters stayed asleep. Now she hoped Aleksis stayed asleep.

When she reached the attic stairwell, strains of "I'm Dreaming of a White Christmas" met her ears.

Uh-oh.

The quicker she learned how to turn off Bow's music, the better.

Quietly opening the door, Rilla started to tiptoe inside.

Then froze.

On the bed, sitting in a play circle, were Bow, Cranberry, and a very wide-awake four-year-old.

☆ 9 ☆

A True Bedtime Tale

Oh, no!

Rilla started to dash to the bed and whisk Aleksis away from the monsters, but curiosity held her back to watch.

"One potato, two potato, three potato, four," the little girl was chanting in words tinged with a Finnish accent.

She was teaching a clapping game to the monsters!

Bow and Cran listened attentively, paws up, ears perked, following Alek's motions.

"Whoa." Rilla grabbed the doorframe to steady herself, stunned by the sight of the girl entertaining the monsters and keeping them quiet.

Boy, I needed help like this months ago. . . .

Then the enormity of what was happening hit her.

Aleksis had discovered the monsters! She would tell! How could a four-year-old keep such a delicious secret?

Rilla's brain whirred, searching for a plan to halt a pending disaster.

Closing the door, she tiptoed to the bed. Part of her didn't want to interrupt the potato game, yet another part wished she could turn back the clock twenty minutes and intercept the monsters before the girl awoke.

As Rilla knelt beside the bed, a dark form climbed up the quilt on the other side. It was Goblin. Scrambling up to see what was going on.

All three monsters—alive at the same time!

When Aleksis spotted Goblin, she simply scooted over to make room for another monster in the play circle.

Rilla was astounded at the child's easy acceptance. Were four-year-olds so in tune with the world of magic from nursery rhymes and fairy tales and animated movies that they didn't question live stuffed toys?

Amazing.

Rilla rested her elbows on the quilt to watch.

Aleksis smiled at her, sleepy-eyed. "Hi."

"Hi," Rilla answered, waiting for the girl to ask about her strange playmates.

"Are you my Aunt Rilly?" she asked instead. In the lamp's glow, golden highlights shimmered in the girl's red curls.

Rilla couldn't *believe* the child was asking about *her* instead of the monsters. The tiny freckled face gazed at her in awe—softening Rilla's resentment toward twin number one.

"Yes, I'm, um, Aunt Rilly." She waited for the girl to react as she casually added, "I see that you've met Bow, Cranberry, and Goblin."

As she said each monster's name, Rilla took hold of them firmly, hoping they got the hint that they'd better be nice to the attic guest.

Aleksis giggled. "Your toys can play."

"Yes. My toys can play." *Such a simple explanation.*

"Are you sleepy?" Rilla asked.

The girl nodded, absently petting Cranberry's head like a dog's.

Rilla prayed Cran wouldn't breathe on Alek's arm. It'd be tough to explain to the grown-ups how the girl's pink sweatshirt had gotten scorched. But the monster's eyes were half closed and he was dragon-purring.

"Let's get tucked into bed," Rilla chirped, "and I'll tell you a bedtime tale."

"Can the toys come, too?"

Rilla doubted the monsters would stay on the bed. They all had preferred sleeping spots. "Oh, no. Cran's bed is in the towel cabinet. Gob sleeps under the rocker, and Bow sleeps on top of the dresser."

Rilla tucked Aleksis back in bed, then went into the bathroom to brush her teeth and change into her leaf-patterned rain forest pajamas.

When she returned, four heads lay on the pillow, waiting for a bedtime story. One gold-red, one Christmas red, one burgundy, and one gray.

Geez. The monsters want to hear a story, too?

Clicking off the lamp, Rilla attempted to climb into bed, but there wasn't much room. She sighed. *No one would ever believe this—except Joshua.*

"Tell me a story," Aleksis said. "You promised."

Monster gibberish seconded the request.

Rilla squinted at moon rays slanting across the walls as she frantically invented a story in her mind. "Once upon a time," she began, "there was a beautiful princess who lived in the highest tower of a castle. With windows all around," she added, glancing at the attic windows.

"What was her name?" Aleksis mumbled in a sleepy whisper.

Rilla paused. Since *she* was the thinly disguised princess in the castle tower, it would be shameless to use her real name. "Princess Hope," she answered, giving her all-time favorite name—the one she used to call herself when she was eight and went through her "I-hate-my-name" stage.

"Princess Hope was in love with a prince named Josh—um, Banks. Prince Banks," she finished, groaning to herself.

"Did they get married?"

Whoa, not so fast. Rilla reminded herself that Aleksis had weddings on her mind since she'd just attended one at home and was here to attend another.

"Alas," she said (since characters in fairy tales talk that way), "the princess was locked in the castle tower with twelve monsters."

Instantly the three in the bed began to jabber and point.

Aha, they see through my fairy tale.

Aleksis giggled. "The toys like your story. What happened next?"

"Well, the princess waited for Prince Banks to come and rescue her from the monsters."

"Were the monsters mean to her?" The tiny voice was fading into slumber.

"Oh, no," pipped Rilla. Suddenly the tale blurred between fact and fiction. *Mean? No. Grumpy? Yes. Lovable and needy? Absolutely.*

And rescuing? She didn't need rescuing. Not by Joshua or anybody else. She rather liked living in the castle tower with her monsters.

Aleksis said no more. One by one, the monsters crawled off to their own beds.

Rilla settled against the pillow to gaze at the moon sliver, floating in the sky.

Forget the prince and princess. A bigger conflict in her true bedtime story was—how could she keep Aleksis from telling the grown-ups what happened tonight?

Were fairy tales always this complicated?

✰ 10 ✰

The Strange Behavior of Sparrow H. Earth

"Calm down."

Mrs. Welter's soothing voice made Sparrow stop hyperventilating and slump into the nearest desk in the classroom.

It was early. Rilla had been up since five. That's when Aleksis woke and started bouncing on the bed.

In morning's light, all had looked normal in the attic. Rilla wasn't sure if the monsters were asleep— or stuffed. Regardless, she hustled Aleksis downstairs. Maybe the child would think last night was all a dream.

I-hope-I-hope-I-hope, Rilla chanted to herself.

Still wearing her rain forest pajamas, she nibbled an apricot muffin while feeding the fish and the kea, who kept saying, "Bite? Bite? Bite?" Rilla wondered if he was asking for a bite of the muffin or her finger.

Mrs. Welter had rushed to Harmony House to organize Sparrow's part of today's lessons after

Sparrow had phoned in a panic about wedding guests arriving earlier than expected.

Rilla couldn't believe Mrs. Welter could be so together at sunrise. She wore a pumpkin sweater over matching leggings. Even her boots were creamy orange. Hair curled and sprayed into place, makeup flawless (pumpkin eye shadow), and pale orange nail polish.

Sparrow, still slumped in the chair, wore a bathrobe over yesterday's sweats. Hair? Hadn't been combed. Nails? Don't ask.

"I have to finish sewing the dresses," Sparrow was mumbling, "decorate the house, figure out food for the weekend, bake—"

"Stop worrying," Mrs. Welter interrupted. "I officially relieve you of your duties as a home-schooling mom until, well, until next year."

"Are you certain?"

Mrs. Welter patted her coifed-to-the-max hair. "Until holiday break, we'll focus mainly on our astronomy project since we've finished up the other units. Nothing I can't handle alone."

Relief smoothed Sparrow's wrinkled brow. "Thank you for understanding."

Rilla sprinkled muffin crumbs into the trash. She'd never seen her mother act so agitated.

"Soon Mother Lapis Lazuli will be here," Sparrow continued. "She's always such a help to me."

The mention of Mother Lazuli's name turned the apricot muffin into stone in Rilla's stomach. How could she forget? Sparrow's mentor would be arriving for the wedding—along with her dippy daughter, Plum.

Rats. What a way to ruin Christmas.

"First things first," Sparrow said, coming to life. "Rilla, go get dressed. I may need help serving breakfast to the troops. Meanwhile I'll be out in the barn if you need me."

"In the barn? But *I'll* feed the cats and Taco. You don't—"

"I'm not going to the barn to feed the animals." Sparrow batted at loose hairs hanging in her face and gave Rilla a sheepish look. "I've been, er, working out on your aunt's, uh, weight machine ever since . . . well, for a few months." She laughed, acting embarrassed to be caught in an act of self-improvement.

Rilla's jaw fell open. Sparrow? Lifting weights? That was the *last* thing she expected her mother to do.

There could be only one explanation.

David Pinowski.

Was Sparrow trying to regain her girlish figure before her former husband arrived? Was this the reason she'd been so crabby and stressed and impossible to live with?

Wow. Sparrow is as vain as Aunt Poppy. Who'da known?

Mrs. Welter began to shuffle papers. Sparrow departed for the barn. Grabbing another muffin, Rilla wandered to the parlor before going upstairs to dress.

The twins were sprawled on the carpet, playing games Aunt Poppy kept in the parlor cabinet for guests and children. Chutes and Ladders seemed to be this morning's choice while cartoons blared in the background. Elias, also blessed with red curls and freckles, was sitting in his underwear, twirling the spinner before taking his turn.

No need to baby-sit. The twins could entertain themselves.

When Rilla arrived in the attic, *"Fa-la-la-la-la, la-la-la-las"* pained her ears. Bow was perched on a window ledge, munching pine needles collected from the evergreens out back.

"Morning," Rilla said, wondering if the monster would allow herself to be picked up. *I've got to find her volume control—if she has one.*

" 'Tis the season to be jolly," answered the monster. Or at least the words emanated from somewhere deep inside her.

"Can you keep the music down?" Rilla asked politely.

"DON WE NOW OUR GAY APPAREL."

"No!" Rilla was tempted to throw the bed quilt over Bow to muffle the music. "How come when I ask you to turn the music *down*, you turn it *up*?"

Instantly the music grew softer.

Confused, an idea popped into Rilla's brain. "Can you turn the music up, please?" she asked.

"Toll the ancient yuletide carol."

Ha! Bow wasn't misbehaving after all. She simply had her "ups" and "downs" reversed. "Louder!" Rilla cried.

"Fa-la-la-la-la, la-la-la-la."

Spontaneously she lifted Bow off the windowsill and hugged her.

The monster didn't flinch or struggle to get away. Pleased, Rilla held her tight. She hadn't been able to bond much with Bow since she seemed to be "off" more than she was "on."

Same with the other two monsters. They were here, yet not here. Plus Goblin was too aloof to let Rilla cuddle him, and Cran, while willing to be petted, could, in a fit of playfulness, scorch the hair right off her arm. So around him, she was cautious.

Rilla danced Bow around the rug, humming along with the Christmas carol playing at a safe volume in the monster's tummy. *Maybe I can survive the month of December without guests complaining about loud music in the attic.*

Suddenly the humming caught in Rilla's throat.

How can I feel joyful when grouchy Mother Lazuli—with her psychic gift of Sight—is on her way to Harmony House?

Last visit, the woman came within an inch of discovering Rilla's monsters. And she was sooooo mean about it.

Bummed, Rilla set Bow on the floor and headed for the shower.

What should she do? Pray for snow so deep, no planes could land? A blizzard so intense, no taxis could make it to Harmony House?

For lack of a better plan, Rilla began to pray.

✩ 11 ✩

Monster Morning

Stepping from the shower, Rilla grabbed yesterday's towel since Cranberry was snoring tiny monster snores in the towel cabinet. No way could she yank a towel from beneath the monster without startling him, and startled monsters often woke up hissing— much like startled cats.

Only this one hissed fire.

Better hurry. Sparrow and Aunt Poppy had to serve breakfast to the B & B guests, the Tamerows, and José, plus fix a midmorning snack for the home-schoolers.

Rilla slipped into a bathrobe, clicked on the hair dryer, then instantly shut if off. What was that noise?

Tap, tap, tap.

Someone was knocking at the attic door!

Was her life doomed to one crisis after another? Setting down the hair dryer, she stepped to the door, barely opening it.

Minna, already dressed, hair pulled up in a frizzy ponytail, stood in the attic stairwell.

"Morning, love," she said. "I'm getting the twins dressed but can't find Alek's shoes. Did she leave them here?"

Oops. Rilla'd been in such a hurry to get Aleksis out of the attic this morning, she'd forgotten her shoes.

But if she opened the door any wider, Minna would see Bow lounging on the bed, nibbling a white ribbon, and Goblin crawling along the baseboard, searching for breakfast spiders.

"Um, I'll find them." Rilla slammed the door in Minna's face, knowing it was rude. Quickly she searched the floor around the bed. One shoe. Where was the other?

She shook out the quilt, bouncing Bow onto the floor.

"OH, THE WEATHER OUTSIDE IS FRIGHTFUL."

"Hush!" Rilla implored—then remembered. "I mean, *louder*, Bow, turn it up."

"But the fire is so delightful."

"Thanks." Rilla hurried back to the door, thrusting out one shoe. "This is all I can find right now. I'll bring the other one down to breakfast."

Minna raised her brows in bewilderment. "If you let me in, I'll help you look."

"No! I mean, um, my room's a mess, and I'm not

dressed, and . . ." Rilla gave the woman a pleading look. "If I don't hurry, Sparrow will yell at me. Please let me bring the other shoe down in a minute?"

Minna studied her for a moment. "Fine, love. Have it your way."

Closing the door, Rilla slumped against it. Close call.

She dried her hair, then hurried to the closet to dress. Bow had climbed back onto the bed to finish her white ribbon.

Wait a minute. I don't remember giving her a white ribbon.

Rilla ran to the bed and whisked it out of the monster's paws. "This isn't a ribbon. It's a shoelace."

The monster made a gagging sound, as if she'd wondered why the ribbon had tasted so awful.

Rilla held it up. One end was frayed and soggy. "Gross!" She dropped it onto the quilt. "Okay, Bow, where's the rest of the shoe?"

Ignoring Rilla, the monster bounded off the bed and climbed onto the rocker to reach the window ledge and finish off the pine needles.

Then she did something odd. She looked straight at Rilla and pointed toward the bathroom, jabbering in monster language.

Was Bow tattling? Mmm. This could be useful.

Rilla tiptoed into the bathroom and opened the towel cabinet.

Cranberry's sleeping head rested on top of a w
tennis shoe decorated with tiny reindeer.

Rilla inched her hand toward the shoe, trying to
be brave.

One, two, three . . .

In a flash, she snatched the shoe away and
slammed the cabinet.

THOOMP! KER-BLAMPH!

Rilla gingerly cracked the door. Smoke drifted out.

She peeked inside. Cran bared his fangs and claws
at her.

"Don't you dare! I'm the one who feeds you." She
waggled the shoe at him. "You stole this, and I'm
giving it back to its owner."

Cran tilted his head, as though thinking over the
food part of her argument. He sheathed his claws
and closed his jaws.

"That's better," Rilla said. "I'll bring you apple
cider at break."

He gave a tiny gurgle as if that pleased him.

Rilla trudged to the closet to finish dressing.

So many adventures this morning—and it wasn't
even eight o'clock.

Something told her it was gonna be a loooooong
day.

By the time Rilla arrived downstairs, breakfast was in full swing.

Aunt Poppy and José served B & B guests in the dining room while Sparrow flipped her famous seven-grain pancakes in the kitchen.

The twins jabbered and jabbed at each other—a lot like the monsters.

Minna had brought a jar of cloudberry jam from Finland because the kids liked it. She spread the jam on their pancakes while a flustered Mr. Tamerow poured their milk—managing to get most of it *inside* the glasses.

"Rill, please take breakfast to Mrs. Welter," Sparrow said, looking almost as flustered as Mr. T.

Rilla lifted the tray Sparrow had prepared and headed into the classroom. Mrs. Welter was at the computer, printing out worksheets.

"Breakfast is served," Rilla quipped.

Yawning, Mrs. Welter leaned around Rilla to squint at the wall calendar. "How many school days till holiday break?"

Rilla didn't even have to look at the calendar. "Only eight."

"Thanks, kid. I needed to hear that."

Rilla chuckled. Nice to know teachers counted down to vacations, too.

Borrowing a chair from the classroom, she carried it back to the kitchen and squeezed in between Mr. T. and Aleksis. Accepting the next batch of pancakes, Rilla ate quickly since there was mail to fetch and barn animals to feed before the home-schoolers arrived.

She tried to follow the twins' conversation, but their accents and unfamiliar dialect made it difficult.

"Right, Aunt Rilly?" Aleksis asked, poking her arm.

"Right, what?"

"Bow played with me, then Cranberry came and wanted to play."

Rilla choked on her milk. *Hush!* her mind shouted. *Don't tell!*

"Who is Bow?" Elias demanded. "And who is Cranberry?"

The grown-ups stopped eating to stare at Aleksis and Rilla.

"Toys," Aleksis answered.

Rilla's hand shook as she set down her glass.

"You played with Rilla's toys?" Mr. Tamerow asked, talking slow and enunciating clearly—like a kindergarten teacher.

Alek's chin was smeared with jam. "Uh-huh."

"Splendid!" Mr. T. exclaimed. "Did she tell you a bedtime story, like she promised?" He winked at Rilla.

"Uh-huh. The toys listened, too, and they liked Aunt Rilly's story."

Laughter rippled around the table.

Laughter is good, Rilla thought.

Aleksis acted miffed. She stuck out her tongue at Elias, who was making silly faces at her. "Tell them, Aunt Rilly," she said. "Tell them 'bout Goblin climbing up on the bed 'cause she wanted to play, too."

"Goblin?" repeated Elias.

Rilla gave everyone a big grin, then winked like Mr. Tamerow. "It's absolutely true!" she exclaimed.

More laughter.

"Well, it is," Aleksis whined.

Minna reached across the table to lift the girl's fork and put it back into her hand. "Finish your 'cakes, love. We're going to the zoo today. Won't that be fun?"

"Yay!" cheered Elias, winning a smile from his twin.

Relief gushed through Rilla.

She'd told the truth, and it had saved her.

Fifteen minutes later, the mail had been fetched and the animals fed.

Joshua was the first home-schooler to arrive. Rilla met him in the foyer and introduced him to the Tamerow family as they marched out the door for a day of sightseeing.

"Well?" Joshua whispered as soon as the coast was clear.

Rilla knew what he meant—and his timing was perfect. "Yes, Bow is awake this morning."

"Can I meet her?"

Rilla glanced at her watch. "Gotta be fast. Every-one will be here any second."

Joshua tore up the stairway to the green floor.

Rilla followed. "Slow down!" she called after him. "Don't run or—"

As Joshua turned his head to answer, Aunt Poppy backed out of suite G-4, running the vacuum cleaner.

A collision was inevitable.

Clicking off the vacuum, Aunt Poppy rubbed her crunched elbow.

Joshua looked mortified. "Oh, Ms. Earth! Did I hurt you?"

"Not much," she teased. "What are you two doing up here? Isn't class about to start?"

On cue the doorbell rang, announcing the arrival of the others.

Rilla frowned at the vacuum cleaner, trying to come up with a good excuse for heading to the attic with Joshua at class time.

"We're, uh, going to carry some chairs downstairs," Joshua began.

"Yeah," Rilla added, following his lead. "Not enough chairs for all these newcomers." She beamed at her one true love, admiring his brilliance.

Aunt Poppy bought it. "Well, hurry. No need to stress out your mother by being late to class."

"She's not teaching anymore this semester. Mrs. Welter let her off the hook."

Aunt Poppy's eyebrows disappeared beneath her bangs. "Oh, yeah? Your mother has time to jog and lift weights but no time to teach?"

Joshua nudged Rilla down the hall before she could answer.

Jogging? My mother? Boy, this is getting serious.

A niggling thought lit up her mind before she could squelch it. *Could Sparrow still have feelings for my father?*

Rilla had never allowed herself to ponder such a thing or wonder if *he* still had feelings for Sparrow.

Unexpected tears made her stumble on the steps.

So why was she choked up if she'd "never allowed herself to ponder such a thing"?

Obviously you have pondered it. A lot.

Up ahead, Joshua paused to wait for her.

Quickly Rilla whisked the tears away. No need for him to see her crying over something that was never going to happen.

☆ 13 ☆

Starlight, December Night

Rilla tilted back her head to take in a night sky that was amazingly clear. Zillions of stars twinkled, like they'd been polished up for Christmas.

Her hood slipped off, letting tucked-under hair tumble out. Shivering in the cold, she wound her hair into a fat knot, then yanked the hood back over her head.

The home-schoolers were wandering around the backyard while Mrs. Welter adjusted the giant telescope. A few kids from another home-schooling group had joined them to view the December sky.

Rilla kept giving Joshua sympathetic smiles. In the glow of flashlights lighting up the yard, he still looked disappointed over what happened this morning. Or rather, what *didn't* happen. By the time they'd arrived in the attic, all was calm, all was bright.

Bow was back to her stuffed state. Just like that.

Rilla assured Joshua that all three monsters had

been active the previous twelve hours, but the way he'd looked at her made her wonder if he thought she was goofing on him.

Soft strains of "You'd better not cry, you'd better not pout" floated in the still air. At first Rilla thought it was Bow, but it was Marcia, singing to Milk Dud, snuggled warm and tight in Tina's jacket.

Wally joined in, his voice cracking. Then Joshua turned the lyrics into "You'd better not meow, you'd better not growl."

The visiting home-schoolers stared, making Rilla feel embarrassed by her little group. She refused to join the singing in protest over Tina's attachment to Milk Dud and the way she'd renamed him "Milky," which fit since his fur was milky white. It exasperated Rilla that *she* hadn't thought of it first.

"Okay, kids," Mrs. Welter called. "Finally got the scope in focus. Lots of falling stars tonight—an unusual number. If one zips across the sky while you're looking through the eyepiece, it means you'll have good luck for the rest of the year."

Wally scoffed. "And that would be, what? A few weeks? Big deal."

Mrs. Welter shot him a withering look in the flashlight's beam. "One at a time now. First have a look at the northern sky, where the comet will appear. See if you can pinpoint what constellations are visible in that direction."

Rilla could spot one constellation without

looking through the telescope. Orion. Locating the slanted star belt was easy.

"There's Orion!" Wally hollered before Rilla had a chance to say it.

"Know-it-all," she griped, nudging him playfully. He gloated.

"Next we'll scan the entire sky," Mrs. Welter told them. "What planets should be visible to us?"

"Mars," Marcia answered. "And Venus."

"Jupiter and Saturn," Wally added.

"Any others?"

"No," answered one of the kids in the other group. "Too far for the naked eye to see."

"This isn't a naked eye," argued another, patting the telescope.

Everyone took a turn, *ooh*ing and *aah*ing at the clarity of the magnified heavens.

The back door slammed and José wandered out, guitar slung over one shoulder.

Rilla offered him a peek at the stars. "Where's your bride-to-be?" she teased.

Placing one hand over his left eye, José glued his right eye to the viewer. "She and your mom are working on the wedding dress and taking turns on the treadmill."

"Treadmill?" Rilla repeated. "I didn't know we owned a treadmill."

"They borrowed mine," said Mrs. Welter.

Rilla waited, but Tina didn't zip in with a snide remark. Either she'd run out of insults aimed at the Earth family—or Milk Dud was softening the edges of her grating personality.

José sat on a garden bench near the greenhouse and began to strum the guitar, serenading the home-schoolers with star songs—"Twinkle, Twinkle, Little Star", "Starry, Starry Night", "Good Morning, Starshine"—plus a silly song he made up to the tune of "I've Been Working on the Railroad":

> *I've been looking through my te-e-e-l-l-l-lescope*
> *all this home-school day.*
> *I've been watching stars and planets,*
> *along the Milky Way.*
>
> *Can't you see the comet coming?*
> *Trailing from night till day.*
> *Boy, we're freezing in our night class.*
> *We'd better get an A.*

José took a bow while the home-schoolers applauded.

"Would you look at that?" Mrs. Welter cut in, pointing to the heavens. "I've never seen so many falling stars."

"Is it my singing?" José quipped, strumming a flat chord.

Mrs. Welter laughed. "*Something* is causing strange things to happen up there. One astronomer even said star patterns were shifting—that hasn't happened since the fifteenth century."

She stepped aside to let Wally take a look. "Speaking of the fifteenth century, how did people back then explain comets and falling stars and eclipses?"

"Magic," Rilla blurted.

Everyone waited for her to continue, but that's all she needed to say. Magic was the only reason she could come up with to explain how stuffed monsters could possibly spring to life.

While Joshua took his turn at the telescope, others offered various medieval explanations for strange happenings in the sky: demons, gods, omens—and always a fear that it was the end of the world.

Joshua stepped away from the telescope, discreetly motioning for Rilla to follow him across the yard, away from the others. Stopping at the far corner of the barn, he clicked off his flashlight as if he didn't want anyone to notice their absence.

"Do you think the falling stars have anything to do with the monsters?" Joshua whispered. "I mean, the legend is pretty clear on how they come to life. Maybe star patterns are being thrown off-kilter since the eclipse and the comet are due to happen at the same time."

Rilla had been wondering the same thing, yet one question troubled her. "What do you think will happen to the monsters when all these strange occurrences are over?" She wished Joshua could give her a definite answer, but all he said was, "Don't know."

The stress of not knowing when the monsters would be real and when they'd be stuffed was wearing on Rilla's nerves. Maybe an explanation would come in the return letter from Global Gifts.

"Maybe it will," Rilla whispered, wishing the company president would hurry up and write back to her.

"Huh?" said Joshua.

Rilla looked at him, unaware she'd verbalized her thoughts. The muted glow of the moon lit Joshua's face in a tender sort of way.

Stepping nearer, he gazed deep into her eyes with an intensity that carved moon-shadowed creases into his forehead.

Voices near the telescope grew distant. All that existed was him and her, in a moonlit eye lock while romantic guitar music played:

"My kisses will number the stars in the sky. . . ."

Rilla's heart rocketed to the comet and back as she listened to José's mellow voice sing of kissing.

Joshua leaned close—so close, she could smell his

cologne. (He was wearing cologne? Wow.) Thrilled, she wanted the moment to last forever.

"Yeowlp!"

That was Milk Dud, wedged between them, along with the blinding glare of a flashlight.

"Time to go, Josh," Tina snipped in a too loud voice. "We're giving you a ride home, remember?" Her words were for Joshua, but her suspicious glare was aimed at Rilla.

The magic spell had been broken—by the evil witch.

Rilla's embarrassment knew no bounds. Turning, she fled across the yard to the back door, away from the awkwardness of the moment.

Marcia, Wally, and the other home-schoolers were saying good-bye and heading out front, where parents waited in warm cars.

José hustled to catch up with Rilla. "Hey, what's the rush?"

"Just cold," she answered, hoping he hadn't noticed what happened—or what had *almost* happened.

Shivering, she glanced back at Joshua before ducking inside.

He waited with Tina while Mrs. Welter and Sparrow moved the telescope back into the greenhouse. His arms were folded as he stared at the ground.

Rilla would give a gazillion dollars to know what he was thinking.

The lump in Tina's jacket told her the girl was planning to take Milk Dud home tonight. It didn't matter. The poor cat deserved a warmer place to sleep than the barn.

José nudged her inside. "You okay?"

She loved him for asking. "I'm fine."

And she was, really.

No matter what happened with Tina and the kitten and the monsters and her father and the wedding, Rilla would never forget this perfect night—and the way her one true love had gazed at her beneath the starry sky.

Sigh.

☆ 14 ☆

It's Beginning to Look a Lot Like Chaos

"Wrap José's gift in this," Rilla said, handing Bow a roll of recycled paper decorated with elves. The resemblance between the creatures on the gift wrap and the December monster did not go unnoticed.

"Greensleeves" played softly from somewhere inside Bow as she spread out the paper on the floor, pulled tiny scissors from her tunic, and snipped a piece large enough to wrap the brass music stand Mr. Tamerow had found in Hong Kong for Rilla to give to José. It was identical to one she'd spotted in a catalog—but within range of her allowance.

Almost three weeks had passed since Rilla's romantic eye lock with her one true love. Lots had happened:

1. The monsters were popping on and off like blinking Christmas tree lights—driving her batty. Sometimes they stayed "alive" for only a few minutes, not even long enough to eat.

2. The twins had taken over the green floor, scattering toys everywhere. Now that Harmony House was closed to guests, the suites had become playrooms for the kids.

3. Even though the semester had ended, the homeschoolers still came over for night viewing. The comet was due to appear any day, and the eclipse was scheduled for Christmas Eve.

4. Joshua had been acting funny toward her.

The last one made Rilla sad. Especially since she was wrapping his Christmas gift (a nifty game of strategy, once popular in the Roman Empire).

Joshua's strange behavior all had to do with the fact that each time she told him Bow was "alive," he'd rush over to meet the monster, yet by the time he arrived, Bow would be motionless.

Rilla suspected that Joshua suspected she was doing it on purpose—just to get him to come over. But she wasn't.

There'd been an awkwardness between them ever since the Backyard Incident (as she had come to think of it). Would Joshua really have kissed her right there in front of everybody? She'd never know.

Now, whenever she caught him looking at her, he'd turn away instead of smiling. Or he'd catch *her* watching *him*, and she'd feel her face turning the same color as Bow's hair.

What to do?

Rilla glanced at Bow, who displayed an amazing talent for wrapping gifts as if that's what she'd been "born" to do. Except she wasn't good at tying on ribbons. She ate them instead.

Plus, Bow had gift wrapped the radio, a pair of dirty jeans Rilla had left on the floor, her math book—and Cranberry.

Unfortunately Cran came to life before Rilla noticed the lumpy gift on the bathroom floor. He burned his way out of the wrapping paper and scorched the tile. How was she supposed to explain scorched tile?

"Time for my fitting," Rilla announced. She debated over hiding the Scotch tape and gift wrap from the monster, but it was pointless. Bow's paws could open drawers and doors better than any of the other monsters'.

Rilla rounded up the Christmas presents to carry downstairs and place beneath the tree. "Just don't gift wrap my bed," she teased.

Bow jabber-chuckled as if she caught the joke.

Downstairs, Rilla added the gifts to a rather large pile already accumulating beneath the grandest tree in Harmony House's brief history. Mr. Tamerow had borrowed Mrs. Welter's van and taken Rilla and the twins to a tree farm to buy a Douglas fir. The gigantic tree almost touched the high parlor ceiling.

After the holidays, the fir would be planted somewhere on the Harmony House acre, ceremony included.

Rilla paused to admire the foyer and dining room. Sparrow, Aunt Poppy, and Minna had outdone themselves stringing pine boughs up the banister, setting homemade candles everywhere, frosting the windows with fake snow, and filling every space with poinsettias and holiday knickknacks.

It was truly beginning to look a lot like Christmas—or chaos, from Rilla's point of view.

The scent of holiday potpourri followed her down the hall to Sparrow's room. Aunt Poppy's finished dress hung from an antique hat rack. Rilla examined it, impressed that her mother had enough patience to sew on all the tiny pearls.

Seconds later, Sparrow dashed in, dressed in jogging clothes. "Sorry I'm late. Get changed and we'll finish off the hem today." Her nose and cheeks were red from morning's chill.

The sight of Sparrow in jogging clothes was still a shock, although the effort was paying off. She'd had to borrow a pair of Aunt Poppy's jeans because her own had become too loose.

Rilla took her time changing into her bridesmaid dress while Sparrow showered. Minutes later, her mother appeared in a white guest robe decorated with *HHB&B* in teal letters.

"Hop up on the ottoman. This shouldn't take long."

Rilla obeyed, standing patiently while Sparrow pinned up the hem, wet hair hanging in her eyes.

"Knock, knock," came a throaty voice.

Rilla's bright holiday mood withered and died as the owner of the voice stepped into Sparrow's room.

Mother Lapis Lazuli. Dressed in a blue cape dusted with snow.

"Anybody home?" she bellowed, peeling off the cape and tossing it onto the bed as if she belonged there.

"Mother!" Sparrow leaped to her bare feet. "You're here!"

The two embraced. Sparrow almost disappeared in her mentor's embrace. Mother Lazuli, wearing her trademark blue from eyelid to boot, fussed over Sparrow being "nothing more than skin and bones," then gave Rilla a cool stare. "Hello, child," she said in a dull voice.

Before Rilla could answer, someone else stepped into the room. Someone her age with wild violet-tinged hair, a half dozen earrings in each ear, and a shapeless purple dress over purple boots.

"Plum!" Sparrow exclaimed, rushing to hug her as well. "I'm so happy you decided to come for the wedding. Look who's here, Rill."

Rilla felt incredibly stupid standing on the stool in her foofy bridesmaid dress while Plum looked her up and down, snickering.

When Rilla didn't answer, Sparrow shot her a "don't be rude" look. "Say hello to our guests."

Rilla wanted to point out to Sparrow how the guests were being rude to *her*. How Plum had wrinkled her nose instead of smiling, and how Mother was *never* going to forgive her for hiding the monsters during her last visit to Harmony House after she sensed something exceedingly odd happening in the attic.

But it was Christmas, and they were guests, and all Rilla had to do was count the days until they departed.

"Hello," she answered, wishing she could make her voice sound as cold and uncaring as Mother Lazuli's.

✩ 15 ✩

Taking Plum to Karma

Hopping off the ottoman, Rilla hurried to the bathroom to take off the bridesmaid dress.

"Give me a minute to throw on some clothes," Sparrow told the guests. "Then I'll show you to your suites."

Grabbing jeans and a sweater, she joined Rilla in the bathroom. "I've got a great idea. Why don't I put Plum in the attic with you?"

Rilla froze, half in, half out of her *Save the Figgy Pudding!* T-shirt (depicting figgy pudding as an endangered species). "You're kidding."

Sparrow ran a comb through her damp hair. "You girls can—you know—*bond*. Get to know each other. Become as close as Mother and me."

Rilla scoffed at Sparrow in the mirror. "Can't you see it?"

"See what?"

"Plum doesn't like me. She despises me. All she

cares about is her weird school—OWSIC, or whatever it's called—in that strange country."

Sparrow buttoned her recycled denim sweater. "The One World School of Inner Consciousness is not a weird school, and Sri Lanka is not a strange country." She tugged on a pair of new jeans, size eight. "Why don't you think Plum likes you?"

Rilla imitated her mother's *don't be ridiculous* glower. "There are plenty of open suites Plum can stay in."

"I was just trying to cut down on housework. One less suite to clean."

"I'll help Aunt Poppy," Rilla promised, glancing at her watch. "Gotta go. José is driving me to the mall to finish my Christmas shopping."

The minute the words were out of her mouth, Rilla wished she could snatch them back.

"You *have* to take Plum with you," Sparrow ordered, hanging her robe on a brass hook. "It'd be rude to leave her here while the only other person her age went off to the mall."

Rilla squirmed for a whole thirty seconds but couldn't come up with a decent excuse. She slumped on the edge of the tub while Sparrow went out to break the news to Mother Lazuli and Plum.

Her trip to the mall would be totally ruined.

All by the color purple.

The mall was abuzz with shoppers, bell ringers, and choirs performing Christmas carols. Holiday ice-skaters, wearing black velvet tuxedos, zipped across the ice rink, entertaining the crowds.

Rilla loved all of it—except for having to share it with someone who sneered at everything and called it lame. She wished Marcia, her home-schooler buddy, had come to the mall with her instead of Plum Lazuli.

Plum was tall and excruciatingly thin. Rilla figured she'd be almost pretty if she washed off the heavy eyeliner, got rid of a few pairs of earrings, and let her hair grow back to its original chestnut brown. The purple tips drew stares from passersby, embarrassing Rilla.

They passed a toy store filled with wide-eyed toddlers diving into a sea of foam balls. "Oooff," Plum said. "Those stupid kids are bonkers."

Oooff?

"They're just excited about Christmas," Rilla told her, wondering if it was pointless to try and have a normal conversation. "You probably acted the same way when you were five."

Plum gazed at her with purple-rimmed eyes. "Give me a break."

Oh, right. Mother Lazuli probably taught her daughter how to grow herbs and concoct health remedies before she hit kindergarten.

Rilla stepped on the escalator. Might as well get this over with fast. "I have to pick up gifts I ordered at Karma. It's on the third level."

Rilla thought Karma was the niftiest shop in the mall. Hidden behind the food court, this tiny hole-in-the-wall had been the perfect place to order most of her holiday gifts.

Plum shrugged and followed Rilla up the escalator, scowling at the gaiety surrounding them and mumbling "Oooff" under her breath.

Rilla figured that putting up with Mother Lazuli all the time would make anybody crabby. Or maybe the crabbiness was due to Plum's shoes. Rilla'd never seen such pointed-toed boots before. Or such purple ones.

The minute they stepped into Karma, Plum's expression softened. The store was definitely New Age. Rilla supposed that appealed to her.

"Miss Earth!" exclaimed the owner, Mr. Peabody. He looked like a regular grandfather—not someone who burned incense, played Gregorian chants, or sold books called *Meet the You You Were in Your Last Past Life!*

Mr. Peabody disappeared behind a curtain to gather Rilla's purchases. Plum wandered the shop, mumbling. Rilla couldn't tell if the remarks were snide or otherwise.

Mr. Peabody returned with an armload of packages. "I will show you everything, and if it meets your approval, Machika will gift wrap for you."

A girl peeked between the curtains and waved at Rilla.

Mr. Peabody opened a gift box. Plum peeked over Rilla's shoulder.

"For your mother, a rock from the Ganges River. A rock that has weathered each season and been smoothed by years of friction. Inscribed with a single, powerful word: PEACE."

"Far out!" cried Plum, making Rilla jump. The girl looked at her with renewed interest and a hint of respect.

Because of a rock?

"You think so?" Rilla said, then kicked herself. She didn't need Plum's approval.

"Can I get one for Lapis?"

Rilla had to remind herself that Plum called her mother by her first name, too.

Mr. Peabody gazed at Plum over the top of his glasses. Rilla wondered what he was thinking. "We can order a Ganges rock for you, too, but I'm afraid it wouldn't arrive in time for Christmas."

That pleased Rilla. She'd feel dumb giving Sparrow the same gift Plum gave Mother Lazuli. *Besides, I thought of it first.*

"Is that all you're giving your mom?" Plum asked. "A rock?"

Rilla wasn't sure if she was trying to be funny or sarcastic. "No. I also got her a whole-grain cookbook to go with the bread maker José and Aunt Poppy plan to give her."

Mr. Peabody put the PEACE stone back into the box and passed it through the curtain to Machika. He opened the next package. "For your aunt."

Plum made a gagging noise, not unlike the noises monsters made. "What is it?"

Rilla chuckled at her stunned expression. "They're called DooDooDogs. Dogs made out of . . . well . . . manure. Aunt Poppy can set these in the greenhouse, and they'll fertilize the vegetables and flowers every time the automatic sprinklers turn on."

Plum contemplated her in amazement.

"I need to get Aunt Poppy something else, too," Rilla said, giving Plum a sly look. "I feel funny giving her *only* doodoo for Christmas."

Mr. Peabody laughed. Plum rolled her eyes.

"Hey," he said, snapping his fingers. "I have just the gift for a soon-to-be-married aunt." He disappeared behind the curtain.

Rilla refrained from telling him Aunt Poppy's wedding would be her fifth, so whatever he came up with had better be mighty special.

If Marcia were here, Rilla would have whispered, "Pay no attention to the man behind the curtain," and Marcia would've giggled and renamed Mr. Peabody Mr. Wizard. Trying to make Plum laugh was a lost cause.

Mr. Peabody returned. "Just got this in from Tibet." Opening a box, he lifted out a copper necklace. "Tibetan folklore claims that copper protects the one who wears it from all things negative. And the links are shaped like hyssop leaves, believed to cleanse the body and spirit."

Rilla peeked at the price tag and flinched.

"I will discount it," Mr. Peabody said, "due to your other purchases." Whisking a pencil from behind one ear, he changed the price.

Rilla felt obligated to nod her approval, even though the price was still too steep. She'd have to dip deep into her panda bank for any other gifts she needed to buy.

"You girls look around while I help Machika wrap these."

Rilla motioned to Plum. "I'll show you what I wanted to buy for myself, but I probably won't have enough money now." She led Plum to a shelf display that read *Kayapo Bracelets*.

"These are beaded by women who live in the Amazon rain forest. The bracelets are similar to their tribal jewelry."

Plum immediately zoomed in on one made of purple and white beads. "I love it." She smiled (actually smiled!) at Rilla. "Thanks for showing me. I'm going to get it, and if you don't have enough money, I'll lend you some."

"Really?" *Why?* she added to herself.

Maybe she thinks you're not such a dweeb after all since you shop at a store named Karma.

Avoiding the purple and blue bracelets, Rilla picked out a green and red one because it looked festive.

"Here we go!" chirped Mr. Peabody.

They returned to the counter to pay for their purchases. Plum had to chip in an extra $6.76. "Thanks," Rilla told her.

Out in the mall, Plum unwrapped her Kayapo bracelet from tissue paper and slipped it onto her skinny wrist. "I know what we can do next."

"What?" Rilla hoped it involved food, like the kind of snacks she never got to eat at Harmony House. Perhaps a heated slice of pecan pie and a chocolate malt at the food court?

But Plum yanked her in the opposite direction. "I can't believe your ears aren't pierced. We're gonna fix that right now."

Rilla almost dropped her packages. "What?!" Sparrow would faint if she came home with a half dozen holes in each ear.

Still, the idea of doing something *without* asking Sparrow piqued her interest.

"All my friends have pierced ears," Plum continued. "You have to do it. I'll loan you the ten bucks and you can pay me back later."

Friends? Now we're friends?

Rilla stumbled through a gaggle of shoppers to keep up with the purple girl. "Well, maybe *one* hole," she mumbled. "One hole wa-a-a-ay too tiny for Sparrow to notice . . ."

☆ 16 ☆

A Gift from
Her One True Love

"There must have been some magic in that old silk hat they found. . . ."

This time the music came from the radio, not Bow. Tonight she was stiff and silent on the rocker with the stuffed animals.

Rilla missed Bow's help. Wrapping the rest of the gifts was taking forever. Too many people to buy for this year. She'd drained her panda bank. Luckily Sparrow had given her money to buy gifts for the twins.

Rilla's fingers kept flying to her ears to touch her new gold posts. Slipping into the bathroom, she admired them for the umpteenth time. Then she fluffed her hair on the sides so Sparrow wouldn't notice. Okay, Sparrow would notice eventually, but why cause her more stress this week?

The ear-piercing session had been weird. Plum, the same Plum who'd refused to talk to her when they were seven on the grounds that Rilla was a baby, actually held her hand and told jokes while the "ear technician" aimed something not unlike a staple gun at her ears.

Didn't hurt much, although Plum seemed disappointed that Rilla stopped at one hole per ear. At least the gold posts came free with the piercing price, so she wasn't *too* deep in debt.

Tap, tap, tap.

Rilla flinched at the knock, then realized she had nothing to worry about. None of the monsters were alive right now, so anyone could enter her attic and it wouldn't faze her. Even Mother Lazuli.

Rilla opened the door without asking the knocker's identity.

Her one true love loomed in the doorway, holding a large paper bag.

Rilla stepped back in surprise. The homeschoolers were meeting tonight for another round of stargazing, but she hadn't expected Joshua to pop into the attic.

"Hi," she said, feeling the dreaded wave of awkwardness. "None of the monsters are up and about tonight. Sorry."

"I came to see you, not the monsters," he said, even though his gaze darted expectantly around the room.

Rilla's spirits soared. "Me?"

He reached into the bag and pulled out a gift. "Merry Christmas, Monster Girl."

She giggled at the nickname, thrilled that he'd brought her a gift. "Come in. I've got something for you, too."

Joshua stepped into the attic and leaned against Rilla's desk. Picking up Owl, he smoothed the tassel on his professor cap. "This is the only one who talked, right?"

"In English," Rilla corrected.

Joshua chuckled, waiting while she found his gift, tucked away in a dresser drawer.

"Shall we open them now?" she asked. "Or wait until Christmas."

"Now." Joshua grinned the double-dimpled grin that fuzzed her heart. "I figured you'd be busy the rest of the week with the wedding and . . ."

Her mind completed the sentence Joshua found difficult to finish: " . . . *the arrival of your father.*" Just thinking about it made it hard to breathe. He'd be here tomorrow. The father she'd never met. *Whoa.*

"Are you okay?"

"Yeah. Sorry."

They sat on the Navajo rug to unwrap each other's gift.

Joshua opened his first. "A game! Cool."

"You have to surround and capture your

opponent without being caught," she told him, pleased at his reaction.

"We can play this with the home-schoolers," Joshua exclaimed. "Wally and Marcia will love it."

"That's what I was thinking." She loved the way he omitted Tina.

"Thanks." Joshua shoved a package toward her. "Now open yours."

It's so big! Pulling off the plaid ribbon, she set it aside to save.

Unwrapping the gift reminded her of all the monster packages she'd opened. Her letter to Global Gifts still hadn't been answered, so she didn't know any more about the Monster of the Month Club than she did a year ago when Icicle showed up in her mailbox. The suspense was a black cloud, fogging a corner of her mind.

Joshua scrunched the gift paper as Rilla opened the box. Inside was another box made of cherry wood with hand-painted evergreen wreaths and an angel—an angel with auburn hair like hers. A wavy banner across the bottom read *Earth Angel* in fancy letters.

"I, um, know you like to keep special things in that cookie tin," Joshua said. "And it was looking pretty full last time you got out the monster cards."

"It's perfect." Rilla traced the letters with one finger and held her breath. She felt like bursting into tears but didn't want Joshua to think his gift had made her cry.

"You really like it?"

She nodded. "Thank you."

Joshua gasped.

"No, really. I love it."

But Joshua wasn't looking at her; he was looking beyond her.

Rilla turned. Bow had sneaked up behind her to steal the plaid ribbon. She bit into it as though she hadn't eaten all day. Of course, she hadn't.

"Hey, look who decided to wake up," Rilla joked, feeling pleased that Joshua could finally meet the newest monster.

He reached to jingle the bells on her cap.

"You'd better not cry. You'd better not pout."

Startled, Joshua yanked his hand away.

Rilla laughed. "I'll show you a trick. Softer, Bow!"

"I'm telling you why."

"Quieter!"

"SANTA CLAUS IS COMING TO TOWN."

Joshua gaped at the monster as she nibbled contentedly on the ribbon he'd tied around Rilla's gift.

"Louder now!" Rilla cried.

"He's making a wish."

"Turn it up!"

"Checking it twice."

Joshua howled. "Let me try."

For the next ten minutes, they played with Bow's inner music. She didn't seem to mind. After she polished off the ribbon, she rewrapped Rilla's and Joshua's gifts.

Clank, clank, clank!

"Oops." Rilla glanced at the clock. "We'd better get outside, or Mrs. Welter might not let us off for Christmas break." Grabbing a jacket, Rilla promised Bow a glass of eggnog, then followed Joshua out the door.

"You got your ears pierced," he said as they headed downstairs.

Rilla automatically pulled the sides of her hair forward.

He raised a brow. "Gee, I never thought Sparrow would—"

"She doesn't know. I was hoping the earrings didn't show."

Joshua gazed at her in awe, as if he knew just how hard it was to go against Sparrow's wishes.

But Rilla wasn't worried about Sparrow right now. She was too happy that she and Joshua were back to being ordinary friends, having ordinary conversations.

Well, maybe not *ordinary*.

Monsters were still their usual topic.

☆17☆

Calm before the Holiday Storm

"We've got scattered clouds tonight," Mrs. Welter said. "But the tail of the comet has finally come into view."

"There!" shouted Wally, who'd brought his own set of binoculars.

Everyone waited while Mrs. Welter focused the giant eye. "Wow, kids, wait'll you see this." Stepping back, she motioned for Marcia to take a look.

"I can see it!" Marcia pointed skyward, keeping her eye glued to the viewer.

"Let me have a turn," cried Tina, shoving Marcia out of the way.

The back door slammed, drawing Rilla's attention. Sparrow. She'd wandered outside three times since the home-schoolers had gathered.

Nervous energy? Due to the imminent arrival of David Pinowski?

Ironically, the more nervous Sparrow became,

the calmer Rilla felt. She didn't know why, but if Sparrow acted cool and calm, *she'd* probably become a nervous wreck. One of them had to remain composed to keep the other unruffled.

While Joshua took his turn at the scope, Rilla intercepted her mother's pacing. "Your hair looks really nice," she said. Sparrow had gotten six inches trimmed off and even let the hair stylist cut wispy bangs. Made her look younger, Rilla thought.

"Thanks." Sparrow wrapped her coat tighter. "Why am I so nervous about David's arrival?"

Perfect opportunity for Rilla to ask the question she'd been dying to ask ever since last spring's mother-daughter missing-father talk. "Are you still in love with him?"

Stunned, Sparrow locked an arm around her daughter's shoulders. Not the reaction Rilla had expected.

"Rill, I was married to the man; I'll always love him. But too many years have passed. You're the only thing we have in common now."

She squinted at the sky. "Oh, look, you can see the comet's tail with the naked eye. It'll be closer and clearer this weekend."

"Don't change the subject."

Sparrow coyly fluffed her bangs. "Guess I didn't want him to look at me and think I've become a *real* Earth Mother. I needed a shove to get me back into shape. It's a girl thing," she added, making Rilla laugh.

"You look great," Rilla told her.

Minna bounced out the door with the twins. The kids were so wired for the holidays, they screamed their way across the yard to play with Taco and the cats. The startled animals fled to safety.

Sparrow nudged Rilla toward the telescope. "Better go take your turn."

Hopping across patches of snow, she jogged across the lawn. Tina was holding Milk Dud so Elias could pet him. Joshua, Marcia, and Wally were turning in final papers on the astronomy project.

Pulling the assignment from her jacket, Rilla handed it to Mrs. Welter and took her turn at the scope. The tail of debris marking the path of the comet shone as brightly as the stars. Magnified many times, the view was spectacular.

"This is our last official meeting of the year," Mrs. Welter proclaimed. After the cheers died down, she continued. "For the next week or so, the comet will be visible without the telescope. The scope goes back to the university tomorrow, so take one last look if you'd like."

She paused to leap to safety as Aleksis dashed past, chasing Taco. "Your final assignment is to observe the eclipse on Christmas Eve. And remember—don't look directly at the sun. Use the cardboard viewers we made."

She stuffed papers into her monogrammed brief-case. "With that, you're free until next year. Merry Christmas, everybody."

"Merry Christmases" echoed all around, then good-byes. Tina stayed behind to teach the twins the proper way to hold a cat. Minna and Sparrow rushed inside to get warm.

Rilla aimed her flashlight beam at the stepping-stones and followed them to the barn. Inside, Oreo was snug in her bed of straw and old towels. She blinked at Rilla in the glow of the flashlight. Taco was circling, getting ready to settle down in the cozy bed Joshua had made for him.

Rilla perched on an apple crate. "This is the calm before the holiday storm," she told them. "My father arrives tomorrow, then it's Christmas Eve and the wedding. After that, he'll leave and go home."

"Maybe next time, *you* can visit *him*," came a voice from the barn door.

Mr. Tamerow pulled up a second apple crate so he could sit and scratch Taco's neck. "I came outside to round up my kids, and suddenly everyone was accounted for except Rilly."

"Just needed to be alone for a while."

He reached to tilt her hand, making the flashlight

shine on her face. "This is all a bit much for you, isn't it?"

She couldn't agree more. "Well, a lot's happened in the past few months." *Even on top of the monsters,* she added to herself.

"A lot's happened to you *and* to me," Mr. Tamerow said. "What do you think of my new family?" He watched her face, looking as though he really cared about her opinion.

"Oh, I love Minna. And the kids. Two of them at once—wow."

"Soon there will be three," Mr. Tamerow said, making room for Taco as he tried to climb between them.

It took Rilla a few seconds to figure out what he was telling her.

Patting her hand, he said, "Rilly, I'm very happy to have my own family, but I want you to know that I'll never forget the way the Earth family welcomed me and made me feel at home at Harmony House. You'll always be very dear to me."

How could he know that was her biggest fear? That he'd become so wrapped up in his own family, he'd forget about her?

"Will you still stop over at Harmony House on your travels?"

"No more traveling for me. I've requested an office job, now that I have a reason to stay home."

"In Finland?"

"No. Here. We plan to buy a house nearby. Is that okay with you?"

Okay? It was wonderful! Leaning around Taco, she hugged him.

"Now," he continued. "Talk to me about tomorrow. How do you feel about your father coming to visit? Are you okay about it?"

Rilla kissed Taco on his wet nose as she considered the question. "Can I answer that question tomorrow after he arrives? Tonight I think Sparrow needs more counseling than I do."

"I've noticed," Mr. T. said. "What's with the new hairdo?"

"It's a girl thing."

Laughing, he rubbed his hands together for warmth. "Let's get inside and find something hot to drink before we freeze out here."

"Merry Christmas, Taco." Rilla tossed him a dog treat she found in her coat pocket. "You have to wait till morning to open your presents."

Pepsi and Dorito climbed into bed with Oreo, creating a furry ball of tails and paws. They didn't bother to say good night.

Halfway across the backyard, Rilla noticed that Tina was still here—sitting on the garden bench. "I'll catch up with you inside," Rilla said, waving Mr. Tamerow on.

Tina's nose was red, and she looked pitiful. When

she saw Rilla, she stood up, acting defensive. "I'm just saying good-bye. I won't see him till school starts again."

Rilla clicked off the flashlight since a full moon lit the yard. "I didn't say anything. Just wanted to wish you a Merry Christmas."

Tina eyed her suspiciously. "Is that all?"

"No."

The girl scowled. "I'm putting him back in the barn right now." She started across the yard.

"Wait." Rilla grabbed her jacket to make her stop. "When I wished you a Merry Christmas, I was giving you your gift."

Tina kicked at a crusty pile of snow, looking uncomfortable. "Um, I don't have a gift for you."

"That's okay. *My* gift can be your promise to give Milk Dud a warm bed and a full tummy and never let him sleep outside on a cold night again."

Tina's mouth fell open. "Really? You're giving him to me?"

Rilla's insides battled. Still, she knew she was doing the right thing. "He deserves a better home than the barn. Taco does, too. I know Joshua wants him. And the other kittens will go to the twins as soon as they move here."

"You mean it?"

Rilla nodded, even though the giveaway plan had just come to her in that instant. Blame it on her self-ish love for the animals. It overruled Sparrow's "no house" rule. With monsters taking up her time, she hadn't been able to play much with the animals. It'd been months since she'd gone to Willow Park with Joshua to exercise Taco.

"Oh, wow," Tina said. "Thank you, thank you, thank you." Twirling around the garden bench, she lifted Milk Dud high. "Did you hear that, Milky? You can come home with me and stay this time."

Biting her lip, she glanced at Rilla.

Rilla let her squirm. She knew Tina had "borrowed" Milk Dud. No big deal. "Hey, I get to see him whenever I want," Rilla said, trying to sound stern.

"Sure. Well, gotta get home." Tina dashed toward the alley. "Thank you! And Merry Christmas."

Rilla waved, ducking her head as she hurried toward the house.

That was a very nice thing you did, Rilla Harmony Earth.

Hush up. It's Christmas. So I got caught up in the holiday spirit.

Still, she'd sleep better knowing Milk Dud now had a warm, loving home.

✩18✩

A Year of Monsters

TODAY IS THE DAY.

Those were the first words that popped into Rilla's mind the instant she awoke. The day she would meet her father. The one who'd left before she was born. The one who'd tried to find her. The one Sparrow had even tried to find. Fate, however, did not cooperate until a few months ago.

In cyberspace.

He was **DCPINOWSKI** and Rilla was **earthgirl7**.

Now she would finally come face-to-face with him.

She was a basket case.

A scuffle in the bathroom hit her ears. *Oh, please. No live monsters. Today of all days.*

Climbing from bed, she hurried to find the source of the noise. Goblin and Cranberry were engaged in a tug-of-war in the bathroom.

Gob's hat was missing. Didn't take long for Rilla to figure out what had happened to it. "Cran, give it back."

Spotting the brim of the hat buried beneath the towels, she reached for it. "Ouch!"

Rilla splashed cold water on her arm to stop the burning. Was Cranberry's flame getting stronger? At first it'd been a mere spark, but now it seemed more fire and less smoke.

And were Goblin's fangs growing longer? Was her fur getting shaggier?

Rilla cleared her too-vivid imagination. "I don't have time for this."

Suddenly Bow skidded into the bathroom, sliding across the tile as though rushing to the rescue. Clutched in her paws were two brightly wrapped gifts. She thrust one at Goblin.

A chittery monster conversation ensued. Gob was thrilled. She gave Bow a fangy smile as she ripped open the gift. Unfortunately it turned out to be Rilla's calculator, which instantly disappeared into Gob's coat pocket.

Cranberry reached for his gift, but Bow yanked it away. Then she cleverly attempted to tease him out of the cabinet with the colorful package.

He fell for it, scrambling out, reaching for the gift with greedy paws.

But instead of giving it to him, Bow hid the

package behind her back and launched into what sounded like a scolding lecture.

Cranberry whined. Bow held firm. Then, with a few choice but undecipherable curses, the November monster handed over Gob's hat in exchange for the gift.

Rilla was so impressed. She smoothed Bow's tunic. "After all the monster scuffles I've refereed in my year of monsters, why couldn't you have arrived earlier? You would've come in handy as a peacemaker."

Bow mumbled a modest reply.

Cran tore into his gift. It was the mouse from Rilla's computer. Within seconds, the treasure was buried beneath the towels.

Oh, well. "Good thing school's out and I won't be needing my calculator or mouse for a couple of weeks."

Rilla herded Bow and Goblin out of the bathroom, then took a shower. What should she wear to meet her father? Mmm. After changing her mind twenty times, she settled on red corduroys and a white blouse, decorated with cats tangled in Christmas tree lights.

She even curled her hair and put on makeup. Not too much or Sparrow would be upset. Just enough to let her father notice she was a teenager now.

Downstairs, pandemonium ruled. Elias had

secretly snitched a gift from beneath the tree. Aleksis had tattled.

Both were wailing after being reprimanded by their parents for stealing and for tattling.

Covering her ears, Rilla wound through a group of José's friends, arriving for the wedding. Aunt Poppy was assigning rooms.

Hurrying past so she wouldn't get drafted to help carry bags, Rilla arrived in the kitchen. Mother Lazuli and Sparrow were having breakfast. Quickly Rilla fluffed her hair to hide the earrings.

"Morning," Sparrow said. "José will be down in a minute to take you to the airport to meet—" She stopped abruptly as if "meet" was the intended end of the sentence.

Mother Lazuli scowled. "I can't believe that man found you."

"I found him," Rilla countered, hating the way she'd called him "that man."

"And he has the nerve to show up for Christmas."

"He was invited," Rilla shot back.

"She's right, Mother," Sparrow said. "Rilla searched for him online through a missing persons service, and bingo—it worked. We invited him to come for Christmas."

"Puh," Mother scoffed.

"He has a right to meet his own daughter."

Yes! Rilla beamed at her mom. For once, she was

defending her daughter in front of someone. After all those times Sparrow had challenged her in front of the home-schoolers, Rilla savored the moment.

Sparrow beamed back. That's when Rilla noticed the lipstick, the blusher, the eye makeup. "Whoa."

Sparrow fluttered a nervous hand, meaning, Rilla assumed, *Please don't mention how I look or Mother will make a big deal out of it.*

"Will you take a breakfast tray to Plum?" Sparrow asked.

"Sure." Rilla glanced at the clock. Almost time to leave for the airport. She needed to eat, but how could she? The knot in her stomach would surely prevent swallowing.

Mother Lazuli put comfrey tea, blueberry scones, and a banana onto a tray woven from tightly rolled, recycled newspaper. "Plum is in suite B-1."

Rilla carried the tray up the back steps to avoid the noisy Tamerow family and arriving wedding guests. She knocked on B-1.

"It's open."

Rilla entered and set the tray on a table.

Plum was lounging on the bed in a Harmony House robe (even though it wasn't purple) and reading a magazine called *Alternative Living.* (Good words to describe the Lazuli family lifestyle.)

"I know something far out we can do today," Plum said, scooting off the bed to pour the tea.

Before Rilla could answer, she added, "But first I'm going to show you something and you have to promise not to tell."

Rilla's curiosity soared. "I promise."

Plum slipped the robe off her right shoulder.

"A tattoo!" Rilla gasped, shocked and enthralled at the same time. A strange purple pattern graced Plum's shoulder.

"It's the Chinese symbol for yin and yang," she explained. "Meaning, balance."

Rilla figured Plum wasn't the type for a fluffy bunny tattoo.

"And look." Turning, she exposed her left shoulder. "My initials in Celtic script."

"P.A.O.L.?" Rilla read. "Two middle names?"

Plum gave her a stone-faced look. "Alpha Omega. Greek for beginning and end."

"Oh." Rilla figured Plum's middle name would have to be something with deep meaning.

Plum untied the robe and opened it. (The purple underwear didn't surprise Rilla.) On her left thigh was a peace symbol tattoo—and her belly button was pierced!

Rilla staggered backward, grasping hold of the bedpost. Wow! She didn't know anyone who'd dare get a tattoo, much less have their belly button pierced.

Plum overlapped the robe and tied the belt. "I

looked in the phone book. There's a tatto
downtown."

Rilla felt as if her jaw hit the floor. "You mean,
you want to get *another* tattoo?"

"Oooff, no. Not for me. For *you*."

"Meeeeee? A tattoo?"

*Me, who's afraid for Sparrow to find out about
measly pierced ears?*

Rilla sat on the edge of the bed, too weak to
stand. "Oh, Plum, I can't. Sparrow would go off the
deep end. What did *your* mother say?"

Plum calmly took a bite of a blueberry scone.
"Lapis doesn't know. That's why you can't tell.
She'd murder me."

Rilla gaped at her. "So you want *my* mom to murder *me*?"

Plum gave her the old disgusted look from years
past. "Are you chicken?"

Rilla met her gaze. She was *not* going to fall
for the "I dare you" bit. She had nothing to prove
to this girl. "I have more important things to
do today."

Plum scoffed. "Like what? Baby-sit two kids who
never shut up?"

"No." Rilla backed toward the door. She wasn't
in the mood to defend herself. And for some strange
reason, she didn't want to give Plum an emphatic *no*
about getting a tattoo. She wanted to toy with the

idea when she had time to think about it. After all, she never thought she'd get her ears pierced—yet she did. A tattoo would have to be tiny, tasteful, discreet, and—*Earth, stop it. You're not getting a tattoo.*

Rilla halted the argument inside her head to answer Plum. "I'm going to the airport to meet my father." She hated the way her voice cracked and wavered over the words.

The scone stopped midway to Plum's mouth. She stood silently, watching Rilla. "But I thought . . ."

Rilla shrugged. "It's no secret. He's never been here before. I've never even met him." Sighing, she reached for the door latch. "Look, can we discuss this tattooing business later?" *Brave of you to say that, Earth.*

Plum dropped the scone and slumped onto the bed. "Go, girl. I don't even know who my father is."

Rilla hadn't expected this reaction. Never occurred to her that Plum could be in the same proverbial boat. "So ask your mother about him. I had to pump information out of Sparrow before she told me the story."

"It's different with me," Plum shot back. The scowl returned. "Lapis never even met my father. It was one of those, you know, test tube pregnancies. She wanted a daughter to whom she could pass along her psychic gifts, and I'm the lucky one—whether I want to be or not."

Rilla absently straightened a throw rug, feeling guilty for being so self-absorbed. "Geez, I didn't know—"

"Not a problem," Plum interrupted. "Catch ya later." Picking up the magazine, she said no more.

Rilla backed out the door. A heavy feeling settled over her heart. Here she'd been feeling sorry for herself for thirteen years, all because her dad was somewhere out in the world. But at least she knew about him and he knew about her.

The thought of some faceless, nameless stranger being her father—and someone like Mother Lazuli being her mother—was enough to make Rilla understand the root of Plum's weirdness.

Suddenly she saw the purple girl in a whole different light. A light strong enough to make the mountain of her resentment begin to shrink.

☆ 19 ☆

The Moment She'd Been Waiting For

José followed a line of cars toward a sign that read *Arriving Passengers*. One hand steered while the other drummed on the dashboard, keeping time to a song running through his mind.

"Go on inside to the gate," he said to Rilla. "I'll park the car and meet you at baggage claim."

She gave him a grateful smile. He must have sensed her need to be alone when she met her dad.

Unclicking the seat belt, she climbed from the car the instant it stopped. Frigid wind rearranged her hair. Entering the terminal, she joined the flow of holiday travelers. Christmas decorations brightened the dull ticket counters. Carols echoed from hidden speakers.

Humming along, Rilla stopped to scan monitors listing arriving flights. There it was. From Portland, Oregon. The flight whose numbers had been burned into her mind. Delta flight 986, now arriving at gate B-8.

Rilla hurried up the escalator stairs, wanting to be there when her father stepped from the Jetway. Wanting to watch his face as he searched the crowd for his long-lost daughter.

Concourse B. She tried to be patient with long lines at the metal detectors, fussy kids, and travelers who seemed to be moving in slow motion.

Stifling the urge to run, she weeded her way between people. Running would make her look like a kid. She was a teenager now. She wanted her father to notice.

Gate 8.

A zillion people waited to greet family and friends arriving for Christmas weekend. Rilla felt invisible in the crowd. Should she elbow her way to the front? Or hang back? Yikes, this was agonizing. Especially since she felt as if she was going to burst into tears at any moment.

Why?

This is it! her inner voice reminded her. *Your father will be stepping through that doorway in a matter of minutes. The person you've obsessed about all your life will be standing in front of you!*

Rilla pulled a photo from her pocket. Not the one Sparrow had given her last spring of the young, bearded man wearing love beads and bell-bottoms and sandals. But a recent picture her dad had sent.

This photo depicted a clean-shaven, short-haired, middle-aged man wearing jeans and a flannel shirt—which seemed appropriate since he worked for the U.S. Forest Service. Rilla stared at the picture. Her first thought had been—he looks like somebody's father. Ha. *Her* father.

Her too full lips and the bony bump on her nose were right there in the photo. Rilla thought she resembled him more than she resembled Sparrow.

The crowd pressed forward as the doors to the Jetway opened and travelers appeared. Rilla studied faces, waiting, waiting.

Then he was there. Down jacket, backpack, hair longer than in the photo. Eyes piercing the crowd with intense scrutiny.

"Here!" Rilla called, waving, but her voice was drowned in the chaos. She'd started to shout "Dad!" but the word had caught in her throat. *Please, Sparrow, don't insist I call him "David."*

Then he was looking at her.

Rilla held her breath as recognition lit his face.

Making his way toward her, he grasped her hands and gazed at her, as a new father might study his newborn daughter.

"Rilla," was all he said. Tears welled in his eyes, and he embraced her for a long moment.

Rilla tried to speak, but unexpected sobs made it impossible.

He held her tight, whispering, "It's okay," into her ear.

Rilla felt humiliated. She was reacting precisely the way she *didn't* want to react. "Sorry," she whispered into his shoulder.

He pulled back. Now he was grinning at her, like she'd just told him the funniest joke in the world.

So much for the mascara she'd painstakingly applied. It was probably dribbling down her face in black streaks. She wiped her cheek, embarrassed, then sniffled. "José, um, Aunt Poppy's fiancé, is waiting downstairs for us."

Her father cocked his head. "Aunt Poppy?"

Before she could explain, he added, "Oh, you mean Sally. Might take me a while to get used to the name changes." He patted her shoulder in a fatherly way. "Let's pick up my luggage. Then I'm taking my girl to lunch."

My girl. This is too perfect.

Grasping hands, they followed streams of people to baggage claim. Rilla spotted José, waiting patiently by the carousel. She waved to him.

The men introduced themselves. Rilla hoped they liked each other. Her wish for the holiday weekend was for everybody to take a clue from the name "Harmony House" and get along. It might be her only chance to feel like she came from a normal family, happily celebrating Christmas together.

Granted, it was a tall order, what with the monsters, the twins, the Lazulis, and the bickering Earth sisters.

José whisked them away to a restaurant that would have appalled Sparrow: barbecued ribs, jumbo burgers, fries, and malts. The kind of restaurant that served buckets of peanuts and allowed customers to toss peanut shells onto the floor.

Parking the car, José turned to Rilla. "Don't tell your mother I brought you here," he warned. "She'd murder me."

Her father didn't get the joke, but Rilla knew he'd figure it out after a meal or two at Harmony House. Wait. What was she thinking? Surely he shared Sparrow's healthy food addiction since he'd inspired her to become a vegetarian. Rilla hoped he wasn't as gung-ho about it as her mother.

José stayed in the car. "You two go have lunch," he said. "I know you have lots to talk about, and once we hit Harmony House, you won't have a moment to yourselves."

The two protested, but José insisted that he'd be back in a couple of hours to drive them home.

Rilla loved him for it. She kissed him on the cheek and whispered, "Thanks."

Small talk kept things moving while they went

inside and ordered. Rilla asked for barbecued ribs since she'd never tasted them. Her father ordered a veggie plate.

She chuckled to herself. *Fear not. My father will fit right in at Harmony House.*

☆ 20 ☆

Thirteen Years of Catching Up

Seemed like only minutes had passed when Rilla glanced up and saw José waiting. She peered at her watch. Two hours on the dot.

While her father paid for lunch, she realized that the once crowded dining room was almost empty. She'd been so focused on the long awaited conversation, she'd barely noticed people leaving.

During the ride home, Rilla sat in the backseat, listening to her dad and José chat. She felt relaxed, as if she'd had a good cry and was wrung out emotionally. The combination of intrigue, pain, thrills, and disappointments made her feel like going home and taking a nap.

Hearing her father's side of the same story Sparrow had told was the intriguing part—how they'd met at a nuclear power demonstration and became inseparable. How they'd married—too young, too quick—and left on their world odyssey.

How thrilled he was to learn of Rilla's impending arrival, and how he and Sparrow had returned to the States for her birth.

Then how the reality of parenthood and mortgage bills set in before he was ready to give up the nomadic life.

That was where Sparrow's story ended. But her father's went on. After years of Peace Corps missions in several countries, he survived a bus accident in Zimbabwe. While recuperating in the hospital, he thought a lot about the child he'd never met—ultimately deciding she meant more to him than trying to solve the world's problems.

He told Rilla how he'd tried to find "Donna and Rilla Pinowski," but the many moves and the name change prevented him from doing so.

In between a half dozen Coke refills, Rilla had cried, he'd cried, then she'd cried again. The waiter must have thought they were crazy, but Rilla saw her father slip him a humongous tip for putting up with them.

The car turned on Hollyhock Road.

Rilla's exhausted calmness began to evaporate. She still had to get through the reunion between Sparrow and her former husband. And if Mother Lazuli said one mean thing, Rilla vowed to plant a live monster on the woman's bed. Just the image of the cranky psychic jolting awake at midnight to find fangy Goblin on her pillow gave Rilla immense pleasure.

The sudden silence in the front seat must have meant that her father's calmness was evaporating as well.

José parked in the driveway. Hopping out, Rilla waited for bags to be unloaded. She couldn't think of anything to say to prepare her father for the onslaught inside, so instead she used the moment to thank him for lunch and for answering all her questions.

When he smiled, she actually caught a glimpse of her own eyes in his. "We're all caught up with the past now," he told her. "From here on, we go forward."

"Get ready," José warned, slamming the trunk. "You're about to go forward real fast."

"Amen," Rilla added. "Did anyone tell you about the four-year-old twins from Finland who've taken over the green floor—I mean, the second floor?"

He glanced from her to José. "You're joking, right?"

Rilla shook her head. "Maybe I should also warn you that Mother Lapis Lazuli is here. Did you know her?"

"Puh," her father answered. "Wasn't that her

favorite word?" He followed Rilla to the veranda steps. "She never cared much for me, but she's harmless. Besides, I haven't seen her in thirteen years. I'm much more charming now than I was back then."

Rilla laughed, suddenly feeling as though she had an ally.

Now if only she could come up with a tactful way to tell him about the *other* surprise hidden behind closed doors at Harmony House—those twelve very unusual "toys." . . .

☆ 21 ☆

The Pinowski Reunion

Rilla felt as though she were climbing the veranda steps in slow motion. She wanted to pull back, keep her father all to herself and not share him.

Mr. Tamerow greeted them at the door.

Rilla waited, watching her father step into the foyer, his eyes taking in the old-fashioned curved stairway and oak banister, the parquet floor, the antique furniture in the registration area. Seeing everything polished and decked out in Christmas wedding finery made the B & B even more grand.

"We're having hors d'oeuvres in the parlor," Mr. Tamerow announced, herding them through the arched entry hung with mistletoe.

The parlor was filled with family and wedding guests. As Rilla's gaze skirted the crowd, looking for Sparrow, she secretly wished all these people would go away and let the three original Pinowskis be alone for a while.

Guitar and dulcimer music strummed above the

voices. "I'm Dreaming of a White Christmas." The music was live, performed by José's friends.

Mother Lazuli, decked out in a blue sequined dress, held court in an overstuffed chair, with guests gathered round to listen to her wisdom.

Plum sat alone in a corner, nose buried in a magazine. She wore a purple-and-black-print sari. From Sri Lanka, Rilla assumed.

The Tamerow twins wore matching navy velvet. The expression on Elias's face told Rilla that being on his best behavior was just about to kill him.

Suddenly Aunt Poppy was there, holding José's hand. "I guess you two know each other," José said, gesturing toward Rilla's father.

"Sally!"

The two hugged and exchanged complimentary small talk:

"How long has it been?"

"You haven't changed a bit."

"Well, you have." (Nervous laughter.)

"Congratulations on your marriage."

"That's what you said the last time I saw you." (More laughter.)

"Thank you for inviting me," he told her.

"It's wonderful that you came." Turning to Rilla, Aunt Poppy hugged her. "How are you holding up, kid?"

"Fine. Where's Sparrow?"

Aunt Poppy glanced around the parlor. "Darn

her. I'll bet she retreated to the kitchen even though we have plenty of food. I'll go find her."

"No." Rilla grabbed Aunt Poppy's arm. "*We'll* go find her."

She understood.

Rilla glanced at her dad. He seemed relieved that he didn't have to experience an awkward family reunion with everyone watching.

"This is the guest dining room," Rilla told him as they headed toward the kitchen. "My classroom is in back. I'll show you later."

Stop blathering nonsense.

I'm nervous.

Think how nervous he is!

Rilla hesitated outside the kitchen door.

He squeezed her shoulder to tell her it was okay. Stepping ahead, he led her into the kitchen.

Sparrow's back was turned. She was sitting alone at the table, sipping eggnog with nutmeg sprinkled on top and reading a cookbook.

It embarrassed Rilla.

"Hello, Donna."

Startled, Sparrow slammed the cookbook shut and came to her feet, smoothing her hair. She wore a red clingy dress that flattered her slimmer figure. Her hair was curled, and her lipstick matched the dress.

Rilla had never noticed what pretty eyes her

mother had. Of course, she'd never seen her wear eye makeup.

"David, you're here."

Rilla held her breath, waiting to see what would happen, waiting to hear violins play softly in the background. Sparrow looked positively beautiful. No frumpy Earth Mother here.

The two laughed.

Rilla frowned, confused. *Did I miss something?*

"Could this be more awkward?" her father asked.

"I . . ." Sparrow began. "You look . . . I expected . . ."

"What? A beard and ripped jeans?" He laughed. "I've grown up. And so have you. Quite nicely, I might add."

They embraced.

Rilla knew she should leave or at least divert her eyes, but she was spellbound.

Pulling away, they faced her.

"How was lunch?" Sparrow asked.

"Great." Rilla shrugged, disappointed by the ordinary question. "Do you two want to, um, be alone? I can leave."

"Don't be silly. David and I have chatted on the phone since you found him online. We've already caught up. It's just a bit of a shock to see someone in person when it's been more than a decade."

"Knock, knock." Minna peeked in the door,

holding an almost-empty punch bowl. "May I come in?"

Sparrow jumped to help Minna and was immediately lost again in her role as house caterer. "Rill, why don't you give Dav, uh, your father a tour of Harmony House? Suite B-10 is all his."

"Thanks, Don . . . er, Sparrow." His face softened when he said the name. Rilla remembered that "Sparrow" was the pet name he'd given to her when they first started to date because she reminded him of a dainty bird, always in flight.

Rilla wondered if her one true love would ever give *her* a pet name.

A *sentimental* pet name, that is.

Something other than "Monster Girl."

☆ 22 ☆

One Big Happy (Weird) Family

Rilla finished wrapping Christmas gifts: for Mother Lazuli, a tea ball made to resemble the earth so she'd think of Rilla every time she brewed a cup of herbal tea. Ha, ha, ha.

For Plum, a pair of earrings shaped like a Celtic cross—now that she knew Plum liked Celtic art.

For Mr. Tamerow and Minna, a porcelain Christmas ornament inscribed with their wedding date. And for her father, a photo album of her favorite baby pictures, school photos from every year, plus family shots of Sparrow and Aunt Poppy.

She'd wanted to gather up captured memories from all the birthdays and Christmases he'd missed. She even sewed a blue cloth cover for the album and embroidered the name *Pinowski* in mauve letters.

After getting ready for bed, Rilla sat at her desk to shuffle through her pile of Christmas cards. Should she open them now? It was tradition for her to hoard holiday cards until Christmas Eve, then climb into bed and open the entire stack at once.

She'd peeked at a few return addresses, pleased that she'd received a card from every home-schooler, including one from Andrew all the way beneath the globe in Brisbane. There was even a card from her second-grade pen pal in Osaka, Japan. Now they wrote only at Christmas.

Resisting temptation, Rilla piled the cards next to the computer and climbed into bed.

Cranberry was snoring loudly. Rilla was miffed at him for burying her computer mouse so deep in the towel cabinet, she couldn't tease it away from him. It would have been fun to go online tonight as earthgirl7 and see what was happening in TeenTown.

Bow was sleeping. Literally. And Goblin was not among the living.

What an odd month this has been.

What an odd year.

The monsters of my thirteenth year rolled through Rilla's mind, like a twangy cowboy song. Perhaps she should write a book about her thirteenth year.

Who would read a book called Monster of the Month Club?

Lots of kids.

Yeah, but who would believe *the story?*

Nobody. Nobody would ever believe it.

R-i-i-i-i-i-ing!

"One, two, three, four, five," Rilla whispered, counting the seconds until . . .

Clank, clank, clank!

The call was for her. She'd phoned Joshua earlier and was waiting for him to call back.

Rilla picked up the guest phone she'd snitched from the second-floor landing. "Hello?"

Her one true love bid her Merry Christmas. "So tell me all about it," he added.

Arranging the quilt, she described meeting her father and the events of the day. "Dinner tonight was strange," she told him. "We ate in the guest dining room, which we never do. My poor father got the third degree from everyone until he'd told his life story twelve times.

"I gave him a fast tour of Harmony House before Mr. Tamerow conducted a walking tour of the neighborhood to look at Christmas lights. The whole time Aleksis kept begging me to let her play with my wiggly toys. If she doesn't hush, people will get suspicious."

"Wiggly toys?" Joshua chuckled, even though she was serious.

"Elias spilled gravy in Mother Lazuli's lap, and I think she put a curse on him. He turned pink and ran from the table. I haven't seen him since.

"Then there's Plum. She won't come out of her room to eat, so I have to take meal trays to her, and—"

"Have you heard anything yet?" Joshua interrupted, changing the subject. "You know, from Global Gifts? Have they sent you a renewal notice to extend your membership in the Monster of the Month Club for another year?"

"You asked me that two hours ago."

"Oh, right. But your membership has almost expired."

Rilla shifted the phone away from her earring. *How can I sign up for another year? That would be toooooo many monsters.* "What if they just keep sending them?" she asked. "Along with a bill? What will I do?"

"I'll help you pay for it."

His answer was quick and firm. But she hadn't meant, *"What will I do about the bill?"* She'd meant, *"What will I do about the monsters?"*

BIG difference.

"I'd better go," Joshua said. "See you tomorrow at the wedding."

The wedding. *Yikes!*

Aunt Poppy had invited all the home-schoolers. Rilla had mixed emotions about Joshua being there. She figured her family would humiliate her at least five million times.

Oh, well. Joshua had witnessed their weirdness on many occasions. How much worse could an Earth wedding be?

"Wait," Rilla said. "Before you hang up, I have one more Christmas gift for you."

"But you already gave me something."

"I know, but this is something you *really* want."

Rilla pictured him sitting up with interest, eyes wide, grinning into the phone.

"I'll give you a hint," she added, "big ears, sloppy kisses, and—"

"Aunt Poppy?" he teased.

Ha! "Noooooo. Let me finish. Its name is a food."

Silence.

"You mean it?" Joshua's voice grew serious. "You're giving me Taco?"

"Yes. I've hardly played with him all month, and besides, dogs aren't meant to live in a barn."

"Wow, Rilla, that is so cool."

"Think it will be okay with your parents?"

"Sure. They told me I could get a dog, but I've always liked Taco best."

"And now he's yours."

"Thanks, Earth. You're a good friend."

"So are you."

Rilla hung up the phone and floated a while before she slept. Her guilt over Taco was officially lifted. And after she gave the remaining cats to the twins, she could devote all her attention to the monsters, old and new—if new ones came.

On second thought, she couldn't give up *all* her non-monster pets. She'd better keep one for herself. Oreo, the mama cat. Rilla could never give her up.

That settled, she slept.

While visions of monsters danced in her head.

☆ 23 ☆

Three Monsters and a Wedding

Christmas Eve. Wedding day.

Eight o'clock in the morning.

Snow falling steadily.

Rilla leaned her elbows on the windowsill and watched fat flakes swirl a path to earth. From the attic, she could see the greenhouse and barn. Both were quickly getting buried in white. How could the home-schoolers witness today's eclipse if snow clouds obliterated the sky?

Yawning, she stretched and groaned a few times. She'd barely slept, due to a continuing racket in the attic. The monsters—all three of them—had been going berserk.

Actually, *they* weren't going berserk. Whatever animated and deanimated them had gone wacko.

One monster after the other kept springing to life—hungry and demanding. They'd jump onto the bed to wake their caretaker. Rilla'd lost count of the number of times she'd been awakened last night.

By midnight, her attic supply of monster food had been exhausted. She'd tiptoed downstairs to the kitchen three times to fetch hot cocoa for Goblin, cider for Cranberry, and eggnog for Bow.

Yet by the time she returned with the beverages, two out of three monsters would be back to their stuffed state.

This is getting ridiculous.

Yawning again, Rilla chugged her third mug of cider. Forget the on again/off again monsters. Could she stay awake during the wedding?

Downstairs, Aunt Poppy was alone in the kitchen, stirring a bowl of warm granola but not eating it.

"Where's Sparrow?"

"Went for a walk in the snow. With your father."

The words echoed inside Rilla's head. *With your father.* How could a relatively normal statement trigger such emotions inside her?

Rilla helped herself to a muffin. Pumpkin, with drizzled icing. "Do you think they . . . well . . . like each other?" *Why is it so hard to ask that question?*

Aunt Poppy snickered. "Well, of course they like each other. They used to be married." She narrowed her eyes at her niece. "Hey, wait a minute. You're not hoping they'll get back together, are you?"

Rilla sat down and stuffed half the muffin into

her mouth to keep from answering. The thought was intriguing, yet scary. She refused to let it form in her mind.

Aunt Poppy put a firm hand on Rilla's shoulder. "Whoa, kid. They haven't seen each other in thirteen years. I don't think . . ." She paused, releasing her grip. "But on the other hand . . ."

"Go on."

"Hey, I'm getting married today. Don't expect me to think in a rational manner."

Rilla mentally filed the question away for later. "So," she chirped, changing the subject. "Today's the big day. Aren't you excited?"

"Excited, nervous, tense, you name it." She shoved away her breakfast. "This granola has turned into granite in my stomach."

Aunt Poppy hugged herself and groaned. "I should be used to my own weddings by now. Why didn't we just elope? Would have been much easier on Sparrow. And José. And me."

"And your stomach," Rilla added, pouring a glass of rice milk. "You've got prewedding jitters. I'll bet everybody gets them."

"I *always* get them." She helped herself to a sip of Rilla's milk. "But all I have to do is make it down the stairs and through the parlor without tripping. Once I see José, holding out his hand to me, everything will be fine."

"Therefore, it's pointless for you to get stressed out," Rilla finished, licking icing off her fingers.

Aunt Poppy squinted at her. "What made you so wise?"

Rilla grinned. "I have good teachers."

Aunt Poppy kissed her on the cheek.

"Good day, mates!"

Mr. Tamerow stepped into the kitchen. Alone, for once. It was rare to see him without a four-year-old beneath one arm, on his lap, or clinging to one leg.

"Minna is keeping the kids upstairs this morning for breakfast. We figured you'd appreciate peace and quiet today."

Aunt Poppy jumped up to pour coffee, but he made her sit while he served them both.

"It's your wedding day. I'll wait on you," he said, filling her *Earth—One Size Fits All* mug.

"Rilly, we've barely had a chance to talk this visit. You haven't mentioned those monsters in a while. Are they still coming once a month?"

Grabbing a nutmeg scone, he joined her at the table. "And are they still . . . real?" (Wink, wink.)

Rilla choked on her milk. Last visit, she'd told Mr. Tamerow the monsters were real and that the legend was more than a legend.

But he hadn't quite believed her. Apparently he thought she was a great trickster.

Rilla swallowed hard. "I've got all twelve monsters now. And yes, they're still, um, real." She waited for his reaction, but all she got were smiles from him and Aunt Poppy.

Suddenly she realized Mr. T. might be able to solve a few mysteries. "Tell me how you signed me up for the Monster of the Month Club," she asked. "I'm thinking about extending my membership."

"Mmm." He rubbed his freshly shaved chin, thinking. "I met the president of Global Gifts at a convention in Oklahoma. Odd fellow, really. Looked a bit like a monster himself." (Wink, wink.)

"He told me he was about to launch a kids' monster club and asked if I knew a responsible young person with a vivid imagination who might be interested in being a charter member. When I told him about my favorite young person, he seemed very interested—insisted that I sign you up on the spot. He said he'd get back to me with the subscription price, but later when I tried to find him, he'd disappeared. So basically, you got a nice collection of stuffed toys absolutely free."

Free? Rilla's mind echoed. *Not free at all. Not if I total the amount of my allowance that went toward monster food the past year.*

José wandered in and helped himself to a pile of cinnamon apple waffles keeping warm in the oven. They were left over from the breakfast buffet set out earlier for wedding guests staying at Harmony House.

The back door burst open, and in came Rilla's mother and father. Sparrow shrugged out of her jacket and immediately went to work. "So glad you can all fend for yourself in the kitchen without me."

Rilla took her dad's jacket and hung it on a hook by the door, then rushed to set a place for him at the table, deliberately finding a coffee mug with no pithy New Age saying printed on it.

"You're spoiling me," he said. "You'll have to come visit me in Oregon so I can spoil you."

Rilla looked from him to Sparrow and back again. She'd *love* to visit him in Oregon. "Can I?"

Sparrow cocked her head. "Maybe next spring during break."

Great!

The adults launched into a discussion about the weather and politics and other grown-up topics while Rilla ate in silence. Glancing around the table at all her favorite people, she felt a warm sense of happiness. The loneliness she'd felt a year ago was completely gone. And the anticipation of visiting her father in Oregon thrilled her.

What about the monsters? Who's going to feed them while you're gone?

Oh, right. Maybe Joshua could sneak in the back door in the middle of the night and tiptoe up the stairs to feed them. Knowing Joshua, he'd love such a challenging assignment.

"Look at the time!" Sparrow yelped, drawing everyone's attention. "We've got a wedding to stage. Finish your breakfasts and get out of my kitchen so I can prepare food for the reception."

"Yes, sir!" quipped José, making everybody laugh.

In seconds the table was cleared. Everyone headed to their suites to get ready.

"Do you want any help?" Rilla asked, knowing that she really needed to hustle monster food to the attic.

"Just make sure the dog and cats are fed, then get yourself ready. After Poppy French braids your hair, I'll pin in the ornament."

Rilla saluted her mom's orders, grabbed her jacket, and went out to the barn. Taco was gone, dishes, leash, and food.

Boy, Joshua hadn't waited long to claim his Christmas gift. Rilla felt sad, yet she hadn't really lost Taco. He was a mere two blocks away, in the home of her one true love.

Rilla fussed over Dorito, Pepsi, and Oreo, giving them their Christmas gifts a day early: catnip toys, balls with bells, and a wind-up mouse.

Back inside, she retrieved her bridesmaid dress from Sparrow's room and headed for the stairs.

"Wait," Sparrow called. "While I was out walking with your father, I picked up the mail. You got a few cards." She fetched them from her jacket. "Now, hurry up and get ready."

Rilla obeyed, dashing up the back steps, counting them as she climbed. (An odd habit she'd acquired.) Thirty-seven steps up the back stairway versus forty-seven up the main stairs.

She bounced into the attic, feeling eager to get all dolled up in her fancy gold dress. Tossing the handful of Christmas cards onto the pile next to her computer, she hung the dress on the closet door.

Then she reached for a Christmas tape to play. That's when she noticed the torn cardboard on the floor beside her desk.

Rilla picked up the pieces and examined them. Nibbled bits of a baseball card fell through her fingers. Dave Justice, Atlanta Braves.

She gasped. Baseball cards were the food of choice for the May monster!

Rilla whirled, her gaze traveling the room.

Ka-thunka-thunka-thunka.

The closet!

Rilla whipped open the door. Bouncing a mini–soccer ball against the wall as if no time at all had passed since he was "alive" stood Burly, the sports fanatic monster.

Ka-thunka-thunka-thunka.

Ho, boy . . .

*"WE WISH YOU A MERRY CHRISTMAS
AND A HAPPY NEW YE-A-A-A-A-A-R-R-R!"*

"Bow!" Rilla raced from the closet to the dresser. The December monster, perched next to a small mountain of gifts, was wrapping Rilla's dress watch.

"Hey, I need that today." Rilla snatched it away, then made a quick monster check. Goblin sat in a corner, playing with a spiderweb. In the bathroom, Cranberry was on his way back to the towel cabinet, dragging new loot (a dirty sock).

Taking advantage of the situation, Rilla reclaimed her computer mouse and slipped a clean bath towel out of the cabinet before he could settle in and bury the sock.

All three monsters were active this morning—plus Burly. It both pleased and disturbed her. The former because Burly had been Joshua's favorite. The latter because it upset the pattern.

Never had more than three monsters been "alive" at one time. And it was always the most recent arrivals. Never had they woken up retroactively.

Should she be alarmed?

No! her mind scolded. *You don't have time to be alarmed. Look at the clock!*

Oh, yikes. In less than an hour, Aunt Poppy will be walking down the aisle. I can't to tell Joshua about Burly until after the wedding.

Ka-thunka-thunka-thunka.

Rilla groaned, covering her ears to the noise.

No time now to worry about monsters. It was time to get gorgeous for the wedding—meaning she had *lots* of work ahead.

☆ 24 ☆

Fairy—Tale Endings

"Hold still."

Rilla studied herself in the mirror while Sparrow looped the French braid on top of her head and fastened it with a gold ornament that matched her dress.

She hardly recognized herself, although she liked what she saw. She'd like it better if the dress didn't gap at the top. *Sigh.*

Rilla pictured a rose tattoo on the bare skin beneath her collarbone. If she'd allowed Plum to sway her, the tattoo would be there in all its glory.

Next Rilla pictured the appalled look that would certainly appear on Sparrow's face. It made her shudder.

"So, how long have you had the earrings?" her mother asked in a calm voice as she sprayed Rilla's hair.

Oops. She'd forgotten to hide the posts.

Before she could answer, Sparrow added, "Didn't it occur to you to *ask* my opinion before getting your ears pierced?"

Rilla fidgeted. "Plum can be very persuasive."

"Plum."

In the mirror, Rilla caught her mother's pursed lips.

"I'm so glad you're not like her," Sparrow said.

"Really? But you think Plum is wonderful."

"Well, she had such promise when she was younger. I don't know what happened. Mother and I hoped that sending Plum to school in Sri Lanka would change her in a positive way. Perhaps she just needs another year or two. Turn around; you missed a button in back."

Rilla obeyed. *So I don't have to compete with the wonderful Plum Lazuli anymore? Oh, joy.*

"There." Sparrow buttoned the dress and smoothed wisps of unruly hair. "The earrings look nice with your dress."

Whew! Would now be a good time to bring up tattoos?

"You'll never believe what Mother told me," Sparrow said. "She suspects Plum has actually gotten herself tattooed. Isn't that outrageous for someone whose future career is all about taking the best care of one's body? Mother is truly disappointed."

Nix on the tattoo question.

"Step back; let me look at you." Sparrow's face got all misty. "Oh, Rill, you look so grown up in that dress. A few more years and you'll be off to college and gone from Harmony House."

Her mother's words thrilled her and chilled her at the same time. She smoothed the ribbon on Sparrow's corsage. "You look pretty good yourself."

Sparrow's hair was twisted into a fashionable knot. Her makeup was perfect (causing Rilla to suspect that Mrs. Welter had been giving lessons), and her gold maid-of-honor dress, which matched Rilla's, did not gap at the top.

"Aren't we gorgeous?" came a voice from the bathroom. Aunt Poppy appeared, resplendent in her ivory gown. She wore a beaded cap with a veil attached. Curly hair tumbled down her back.

The three giggled like girlfriends at a sleep over. "Time to head up the back steps and get into place," Sparrow said.

Her words made Rilla's heart swirl like crazy.

"This is it." Aunt Poppy wrung her hands before taking her bouquet from Sparrow. "Break a leg, everybody." Acting silly, she step-paused, step-paused out the door.

Before Sparrow could follow, Rilla grabbed her arm and pulled her back. She couldn't wait any longer to ask the question she'd been dying to ask for the past forty-eight hours.

"What?" Sparrow asked. "Are you getting nervous?"

Rilla bit her lip, unsure how to phrase the question. "I just need to know about you and Dad."

Sparrow shook out the ribbons on her bouquet. "Can you be more specific?"

"Well, you two seem to be getting along so well, and—"

"Oh, Rill." The reality of what her daughter was asking made her step back into the room and close the door. "If you're asking if your dad and I are getting back together—please don't think that way. We're enjoying each other's company. We were always great friends; I've told you that. And it's been fun to catch up and compare notes."

She was quiet so long, Rilla wondered what she was thinking.

"David's life is in Oregon, and mine is here at Harmony House," Sparrow continued. "Besides . . ."

"Besides what?"

"Well, if he hasn't mentioned it to you, then I won't."

"Oh, come on; that's so unfair."

Sparrow met her gaze. "Well, all right. There's someone in Oregon who your father sees on a regular basis."

It took Rilla a minute to absorb that bit of news. "You mean, he has a girlfriend?"

"Rill, life goes on. I may meet someone eventually, and hey, I might even get married again. Who knows? The important thing is that you and he connected. He will always be your father, and now you can have a real relationship with him. That's why it was great for him to come here."

Sparrow enfolded her in a hug. "Please don't expect a fairy-tale ending for us. That's what you should wish for Poppy and José. I think she found the right guy this time for happily ever after."

Rilla tried to take her mother's answer in stride, dutifully burying the notion of her parents reuniting. So much for wishful thinking. Since fairy-tale endings were few and far between, she'd focus on Aunt Poppy and José right now.

Sparrow nudged her out the door. "Come on, you gorgeous young lady. Let's go marry off your old-maid aunt."

Laughing, Rilla followed her up the back steps. A chapter of her life seemed to be ending. The feeling was bittersweet, yet that quip about fairy-tale endings still gave Rilla hope.

And after all, Hope was her all-time favorite name.

☆ 25 ☆

Here Comes the Bride
(for the Fifth Time)

Rilla waited on the second-floor landing. The key to the attic was a lump in her shoe since she'd had to take off the silver chain. She hoped it didn't give her a blister.

Music drifted from the parlor—instrumentals from a preprogrammed tape José had assembled for his own wedding.

Behind her, Sparrow and Aunt Poppy whispered together and fussed with each other's hair and dresses. Rilla glanced back at them, barely recognizing the Earth sisters—*sans* jeans and unstyled lengths of hair.

The improvement was remarkable.

Aunt Poppy's "something old" was a pair of Irish lace gloves inherited from Great-grandmother Knox. Something new: jade earrings from José, one a star, one a half-moon.

Something borrowed was a woven gold Finnish bracelet from Minna. Something blue: a brooch from Mother Lazuli, made of real lapis lazuli, surrounded by tiny moonstones, symbolizing femininity and strength. The piece was similar to jewelry worn by Isis, an Egyptian goddess, mother of all things.

Rilla loved the wedding bands—tricolor gold, intertwining love knots, symbolizing eternal adoration.

Standing stiffly, she clutched her bouquet of red and green carnations, interspersed with holly and ivy, smiling when she recognized the instrumental melody of "Poppy's Song," the tune José had sung when he proposed to his future bride.

Rilla hummed along, admiring the way Harmony House was dressed up for the holidays. She wished the evergreen boughs could stay looped around the oak banister all year.

Below, a pot of poinsettias brightened the registration desk. Twinkly lights outlined windows. Holiday potpourri pots flavored the air with the scent of pine, cinnamon, and cloves.

Outside, heavy snowfall was a nice touch for a Christmas wedding. Couldn't have planned it better. Rilla figured Mother Lazuli probably took credit for nature's perfect timing.

As if the blue woman sensed that Rilla was thinking nasty thoughts about her, she stepped from the parlor. "Psst!" she whispered. "It's time."

"Go, Rill," urged Sparrow. "Remember to

pause at the doorway, walk slowly, and don't run up the aisle."

Taking a deep breath to ward off butterflies hip-hopping in her stomach, Rilla lifted her dress with one hand so she wouldn't trip on the stairs.

At the bottom, Mother Lazuli grasped Rilla's shoulders to position her on the green runner that represented the "aisle." She whispered the same instructions Sparrow had just given, as if she thought Rilla was too dim-witted to remember for more than two seconds.

"I *know*," Rilla snipped, wiggling from her grasp.

Facing the parlor filled with guests seated in folding chairs on both sides of the green aisle, she paused, as instructed. Wow. The room was packed.

Rilla walked slowly along the back wall, then turned to head up the aisle. Everyone was staring at her. Gulp.

Flashbulbs exploded, making her flinch. Her father had been drafted to play photographer. Rilla smiled, ready this time before the bulb flashed.

Step-pause, step-pause.

Joshua Banks, looking uncomfortable in a new suit, gaped at her in awe. It might possibly be the first time he'd ever seen her wearing a dress. As long as she lived, she'd never forget the look on his face.

Next to him sat the other home-schoolers—Marcia, Wally, and Tina, along with Mrs. Welter, dressed to the teeth in silver. Tiny silver bells that actually tinkled dangled from her ears.

Rilla stepped slowly up the aisle, smiling at her father-photographer.

There was kind Mr. Baca, owner of Mr. Baca's One-Stop Shoppette, and his son, Carlos. She even caught sight of the Tonkawa sisters, Lottie and Dottie, who'd installed Harmony House's air-conditioning last summer. They were dressed in identical scarlet pantsuits.

"Aunt Rilly!" came a tiny voice as Rilla passed the twins, decked out in matching Christmas outfits that made them look like snow bunnies.

Minna hushed Aleksis and smacked Elias on the leg to make him stop squirming.

Rilla's gaze skirted the crowd for Plum. Was she behind that purple, wide-brimmed hat? Of course, Plum wouldn't turn to watch the procession because that's what she was expected to do.

Rilla's knees began to shake. She focused on José, standing at attention under an arched trellis woven with greenery. A fat clump of mistletoe hung from the center of the wedding arch.

Beside José stood the best man, Mr. Tamerow. He blew her a kiss.

José's face was as white as his shirt. Seeing him this shook up calmed Rilla down. She crossed her eyes at him. He grinned.

Taking her place, Rilla turned to watch Sparrow step-pause her way up the aisle. Rilla studied her father as he watched Sparrow. His expression was melancholy. Was he remembering his own wedding?

Suddenly the music grew louder, and a jazzy wedding march began to play. Aunt Poppy appeared, looking coy as *oh*s and *ah*s skittered around the parlor. She made it to the altar in three steps. No pausing for her today.

The ceremony was brief but beautiful, performed by a justice of the peace named Rainbow America. Rilla figured it wasn't an original name any more than Sparrow Harmony Earth or Lapis Lazuli were original names.

Then it was over and José was kissing Aunt Poppy and people were clapping and flashbulbs were popping.

Rilla followed the newlyweds down the aisle, trying hard not to look at Joshua Banks to see if he was watching her. (Okay, she peeked. He was.)

The reception commenced in the dining room. Rilla was relieved that the ceremony was over. Now she could eat—but not until she survived the receiving line and a million hugs and kisses, mostly from people she didn't know. (From Joshua, she got a handshake.)

Finally she grabbed a piece of wedding cake and found a corner so she could eat it quickly.

"Traditional weddings are so bourgeois."

Plum, wearing a one-piece purple cat suit, adjusted her hat and glowered at the crowd.

Rilla wondered what *bourgeois* meant, doubting it was a compliment.

She watched Plum's gaze take in her "traditional" bridesmaid dress but refused to apologize for the way she looked. She *liked* the way she looked.

"I'm getting out of here," Plum said. "Want to come? We can go downtown and see what's open on Christmas Eve. Of course, if I was more psychic, I'd already *know* what's open."

Rilla met her sarcastic gaze. Why had she let this person intimidate her all these years? In truth, she felt sorry for Plum. "No, thank you," she told her. "I'd rather be with my family."

Plum scoffed. "Bully for you." With that, the girl slithered away through the crowd. Rilla watched her leave. Mother Lazuli was watching, too. Suddenly it dawned on Rilla that not once during this entire visit had the woman bragged about her daughter like she used to.

Could Mother Lazuli possibly be thinking that Rilla turned out far better than her own dear Plum? Oh, my. Ha, ha, ha.

Rilla spotted Joshua weaving through the crowd. Was he looking for her? Now was her chance to tell him her startling monster news. Finishing her cake, she caught up with him in the parlor, motioning him away from chatty clumps of people so they were out of earshot.

He followed her to the wedding arch. "Guess what?" she whispered.

"What?" He smirked at her. "You're the first girl to get me to the altar?"

Oops. She hadn't realized where she'd led him. Touching her cheek, she willed it to stop blushing.

Meanwhile Joshua was laughing at his own joke. "You look really nice," he said.

"Thank you."

Bingo. Back to those horrid awkward feelings. *As long as we stick to monster talk, we're fine.*

Suddenly Joshua leaned over and kissed her on the cheek, startling her. Grinning, he pointed at the mistletoe, dangling above.

Rilla could have melted right into the green runner. Did he think she'd stopped beneath the mistletoe on purpose? Yikes!

All she'd wanted was to get Joshua alone and fill him in on what had happened in the attic. "I'm trying to tell you something," she whispered, feigning impatience since the kiss embarrassed her. "This morning I found pieces of a baseball card in my room."

"So?"

"Remember who eats baseball cards?"

Joshua gasped. "Burly! Is he alive?"

"Yes. Do you know what that means?"

"Oh, wow. Any of them could come to life. Not just the newest ones."

"Exactly." Rilla brought him up to date on the strange occurrences of the past two days. How the monsters had been clicking on and off like flashbulbs at the wedding.

"Seems like the closer we get to the eclipse, the more it happens," she finished, glancing toward the windows.

Joshua followed her gaze. "Look, it's getting dark. The eclipse is probably starting."

Excited voices in the foyer confirmed his prediction. The parlor emptied as guests hurried to the front windows to watch the sky.

"Let's go," he said.

"Wait."

All those times Plum had called her "chicken" lit up in Rilla's mind. Well, she *wasn't* chicken. Backing up, she motioned for Joshua to follow.

"What?" he asked, taking a step toward her.

Faster than a monster could spring to life, she planted a kiss—not on Joshua's cheek—but right smack on his lips. No chickens here.

"Merry Christmas," she whispered.

Her one true love was far too shocked to answer.

☆ 26 ☆

Mother Know-it-all

Grinning, Joshua grabbed her hand. They ran down the aisle, through the foyer, and out the front door. Rilla was shaking inside over the kiss. But it was a good kind of shaking.

Icy air and whirling snowflakes greeted them, which meant clouds hid the afternoon performance in the sky. Light behind the clouds was fading, so it was still possible to monitor the progress of the eclipse.

A few wedding guests huddled outside with the home-schoolers and Mrs. Welter, squinting skyward. The cardboard viewers they'd made in class in order to watch the sun without hurting their eyes weren't needed on a day like this.

Dusk fell, as if someone fast-forwarded evening. Wally gave everyone a running commentary on how the moon was slowly swallowing daylight as it moved across the face of the sun.

Suddenly the veranda steps shuddered, as if an earthquake had rumbled through the neighborhood. Rilla glanced around, shivering in her flimsy dress. That was odd.

At the same moment, twilight enveloped the quiet yard. Stillness reigned. The only sound Rilla could hear was breathing.

Joshua frowned at her, one brow raised in question, as if he thought the trembling was a bit strange, too.

"Rill!" The porch light clicked on.

Standing on tiptoes, she peered over heads to see who was calling. The crowd parted. Sparrow, a bewildered look on her face, frantically motioned her inside.

Glancing at Joshua, Rilla shrugged and headed for the warmth indoors, glad to be out of the frigid air.

"It's Mother Lazuli," Sparrow whispered, taking her arm. "She's having some kind of, well, *vision,* she called it. And she wants you with her."

Rats.

"Do I have to?" Rilla whined, trying to tug her arm away. "I want to watch the eclipse. It's my class assignment," she added to convince her mother that she was *supposed* to be outside on the veranda with the other home-schoolers.

But Sparrow held firm, cocking her head as if trying to hear something three floors up.

Three floors up? *Omigosh. The attic!* Had Bow turned up the volume of her music? Was Burly still kicking his soccer ball against the wall?

"Did you feel the house tremble a moment ago?" Sparrow asked.

"Yes," Rilla answered. So. It was the entire house, not just the veranda.

"Get going, then," Sparrow said. "Mother's in the kitchen."

"Why does she want me?"

"I honestly don't know."

Rilla *really* wanted to go back outside with Joshua and the others. Irritated, she wove through the crowd in the dark dining room. At the door, she reached for the dial to turn up the light of the chandelier, then noticed Aunt Poppy and José dancing to a soft waltz by candlelight. Ahhhhhh. She let romance rule.

In the kitchen, Mother Lazuli sat stiffly at the table, fanning herself with one of Sparrow's Christmas napkins, embroidered with *Peace on Earth, Goodwill to Women.* How could she possibly be hot when ice was forming on the windows?

Mother Lazuli turned a piercing gaze upon Rilla. "Do you recall when I was here last spring?"

Rilla nodded, remembering how the woman's psychic powers had picked up strange disturbances in the attic. That was the closest Rilla had come to having the monsters discovered.

"I fell ill, due to unusual energy patterns in this house. I only fall ill when the power I've encountered is equal to my own."

Yeah, right. Rilla wasn't in the mood for a lecture. Besides, she never thought Mother Lazuli's "powers" amounted to a hill of organic beans.

She predicted Mr. Tamerow's wedding, didn't she?

Well, okay. It'd seemed impossible at the time but had come true three months later.

And you know *her fascination with the attic has* something *to do with the monsters.*

Right.

So listen to her.

Rilla shook her head to clear it. Was Mother Lazuli taking over her inner voice? Or was Sparrow nipping at her conscience?

"Last spring," Mother continued. "Something in the uppermost part of this house broke harmony with the universe."

Ho, boy. Rilla remembered that phrase—"broke harmony with the universe"—and how it'd washed shivers up and down her spine.

"It's happening again," Mother Lazuli said. "Only on a much grander scale. A scale so large, the strange vibrations I previously received are now coming to me as visions."

"Visions?" *Uh-oh. Can she "see" inside the attic?* Rilla's heart thundered.

Suddenly Aleksis and Elias dashed into the

kitchen, playing chase. Rilla was relieved for the distraction.

"Out!" Mother Lazuli commanded. Yelled, rather.

The twins skidded to a stop and cowered before the woman.

"Hey, guys," Rilla said, hating that Mother had scared them. "Will you carry a plate of Christmas cookies to the wedding reception for me?"

They acted eager to help.

Quickly Rilla arranged a fresh batch of Sparrow's Nutty Squares, giving the twins instructions to walk slowly and not tip the plate. "Serve the guests, then you can each have one."

Speaking of Nutty Squares, Rilla returned her attention to Mother Lazuli.

"My dreams," the woman said without missing a beat, "have been troubled with visions of . . . of creatures. Creatures of color, fangs, a curly tail, many eyes."

Yikes! She's dreaming about the monsters. Fangs would be Goblin, curly tail would be Sweetie Pie, the February selection, and many eyes would be Icicle, the January monster.

"They speak to each other," Mother Lazuli said. "Strange utterings. A language unknown on this planet."

Monster lingo. At least that's what Rilla called it.

Mother's gaze penetrated Rilla's eye sockets. "What do you know of this?"

Rilla shrugged—which seemed the best way to react in uncomfortable situations.

"The girl child knows of them."

"Girl child?" Rilla repeated. "You mean, Aleksis?"

"Her description of a dragon-like creature came right out of my dreams."

That would be Cranberry. Oh dear, oh dear, oh dear.

Say something!

Like what? Anything I say can and will be used against me.

Sparrow stuck her head into the kitchen. She appeared worried and curious at the same time. "Is everything all right?"

Rilla backed up, planning a quick getaway.

"Bring me the boy," Mother Lazuli demanded.

"What boy?" Sparrow asked.

"I think she means Elias," Rilla said.

Mother Lazuli stared at her, vaguely amused. "I mean the boy you kissed beneath the wedding arch."

Gasp! HOW DID SHE KNOW?

Her powers are stronger than you think, Earth.

Oh, stop. She could've been spying. . . .

Sparrow scrutinized her daughter. "Well, *that* could only be Joshua Banks." She cleared her throat in a "We'll talk about this later" sort of way. "I'll find him."

"No, no. *I'll* find him." Rilla lunged toward the door, wanting to get out of there, wanting to warn Joshua about the crabby purple seer.

"STAY!" Mother Know-it-all jabbed a pudgy finger at her, tipped with blue nail polish.

Rilla froze, glued to the kitchen tile as Sparrow hurried to fetch Joshua. There was no place to run. No place to hide.

Think, Earth!

This woman is about to eat you alive!

☆27☆

The Truth about the Monsters

The kitchen grew so dark, it was difficult to see Mother Lazuli's face. Rilla didn't bother to click on the light. Her mind was too busy trying to think of a way to throw the woman off her quest.

A quest for the truth about the monsters.

Joshua stumbled into the kitchen, escorted like a prisoner by Sparrow. His eyes focused on Rilla in the dimness. Bewilderment crinkled his face.

Poor Joshua. He didn't know Mother Lazuli, but he was about to get a quick, unpleasant introduction.

Mother didn't speak. Instead, her gaze bored a hole through Sparrow until she got the hint to leave.

Reluctantly Sparrow returned to the wedding reception. Rilla figured this whole mystery was driving her mother crazy.

Muffled music played in the background. Rilla resented Mother Lazuli for making her miss Aunt Poppy's reception as well as the eclipse. *And* she resented the woman for making Joshua feel uncomfortable.

"We really need to get back," Rilla ventured.

"Silence!"

Mother Lazuli cocked her head, as though picking up radio waves from an alien spacecraft.

"You," she said to Joshua.

He flinched. "What did *I* do?"

"You didn't do anything," Rilla began. "It's just—"

"I'm talking to the boy," Mother hissed, stifling Rilla. She turned back to Joshua. "What do you know of creatures in the attic?"

Rilla thought Joshua was going to collapse in shock. He gaped at her instead of his interrogator.

Rilla shuffled her feet, nonchalantly moving closer to him.

"She's guessing," Rilla mumbled, trying to keep her voice too low for the woman to hear. "Bluff."

"Speak up, child!"

Rilla shot her a clueless look. "I was just explaining—"

Suddenly Minna rushed down the back steps. "Rilla! Come quick!"

Rilla didn't need a second invitation. She was across the kitchen in two steps, dashing up the stairs after Minna.

"STOP!" commanded Mother Lazuli.

Rilla stopped. Not because the woman ordered her to but because of Joshua. She couldn't leave him down there to be grilled by the person who could scare the cape off Count Dracula.

"Come on, Joshua! We need you!"

He was there in a nanosecond, looking mighty grateful.

In the background Mother Lazuli howled threats, but Rilla felt sure she wouldn't race up the steps after them.

Minna stopped on the second floor to explain. "I brought Aleksis upstairs because she has a tummy ache, and I heard bathwater running in the attic but the back door is locked. If the tub overflows, it will ruin the floors and ceilings, and—oh, love, your mother would have a fit."

Bathwater, Rilla's mind echoed. That could mean only one thing. Chelsea, the mermaid-monster, had come to life!

"I'll take care of it, Minna. Thanks for letting me know."

Rilla tore up the steps with Joshua on her heels. "Hope Alek's tummy feels better," she hollered back.

When they were out of earshot, Rilla whispered. "Do you know what this means?"

"The April monster, right?"

"Yes! Do you think the eclipse is causing all this?"

"How could it?" Joshua asked, tripping on the steps in the dark. "The monsters are supposed to be sparked to life by star patterns, not by eclipses."

They paused in the attic stairwell, gasping for breath. "Yes," Rilla agreed, "but remember what Mrs. Welter said about the eclipse and the comet happening at the same time?"

"You're right. She said strange happenings in the midwinter sky were changing star patterns."

Gulp.

Rilla slipped off her shoe to retrieve the attic key. Her hand trembled as she unlocked the door and pushed it open.

What met her eyes took her breath away. Not three, not four, not even five live monsters had taken over the attic.

Without needing to count, Rilla knew her biggest nightmare had come to pass. Every single Monster of the Month Club had sprung to life on Christmas Eve!

⭒28⭒

Happily Ever Attic

Rilla's first reaction was amazement and exhilaration.

She'd prepared herself for a few of the older attic residents to make a comeback, but nothing had prepared her for all twelve monsters living, breathing, and moving about at once.

Rilla's second reaction was: "Lock the door!"

Joshua, a look of complete and utter marvel on his face, whisked the door shut and locked it.

No way would Rilla allow Mother Lazuli to see the miracle taking place on the fourth floor of Harmony House. She'd probably douse the monsters with herbal tea, melting them into the floor like the wicked witch in *The Wizard of Oz*.

"Hey, buddy," Joshua exclaimed, hopping out of the way as Sparkler (the July monster) zipped past on his mini-skateboard.

Whomp!

That was a soccer ball, hitting the bathroom door. Joshua rescued it and tossed it back to Burly (May).

Rilla stood frozen, not sure which monster to greet first. The sound of running water reminded her who needed immediate attention. "Chelsea!"

Rilla rushed into the bathroom. The April mer-monster swam in lazy strokes around the bathtub, splashing water over the sides. Rilla shut off the faucets. "It's full already."

Chelsea stopped swimming to jabber at Rilla, as if greeting an old friend.

Rilla grabbed a bath towel and mopped up the floor. "Hey, Cranberry," she called, knocking on the towel cabinet. "Come out and meet Chelsea." The November monster peeked out to warily study the mermaid. Did water make him nervous? Might put out his flame—ha!

"I'll be back in a minute," Rilla told them, eager to check on the others. In the bedroom, she caught sight of Sweetie Pie scribbling on the wall with a pink marker. "Hey," Rilla yelped, rushing to whisk the marker from Sweetie Pie's paws.

The February monster gazed lovingly at her, making Rilla's heart turn over. She'd been the only mon-ster who really liked being cuddled.

"Ouch!"

Rilla jumped back as the rocking chair crunched her toe. Icicle (January) was buried beneath an oversize book called *The Complete Encyclopedia of Monsters*. Rilla had bought it last summer, hoping it contained information about the variety of which she was most familiar.

"Hey, Icicle," Rilla purred. He was her very first monster. For a whole month, it had been just her and him. He held a special place in her heart—even though he never quite warmed up to her.

"Hrrrmmmph," he said, rubbing his stomach.

He was hungry. Of course he was. All of them were probably hungry.

Geez, how could she feed them all? Wouldn't that be a full-time job?

She gazed at Joshua. He was in the middle of a five-way game of catch with Burly, Sparkler, Goblin, and . . . Shamrock! The March monster was the only one who'd never come to life. Rilla watched him, not wanting to interrupt the game. His green fur and jaunty hat made him look like a tiny leprechaun.

"Silver bells, silver bells, it's Christmastime in the city."

Rilla caught sight of Bow in her spot on top of the dresser. Now the mountain of wrapped gifts threatened to topple over.

"You've got mail!" came a computer-generated voice. Rilla's gaze skittered across the room. Owl! The September monster was back in cyberspace, his favorite place. Who had he e-mailed?

Curious, Rilla made her way across the room, dodging flying balls and covering her ears against monster babble, which was growing louder by the second. Good thing Harmony House was filled with music and guests. Hopefully no one would notice the racket in the attic.

Rilla sat next to Owl and read the computer screen:

To: earthgirl7
From: MissMonster

Yes, I'm married. No, I'm not a real monster. Boy, you ask weird questions.

"Oh, Owl, you're at it again. Using my screen name and getting me into trouble." She pretended to be shocked. "Are you proposing marriage to **MissMonster?**"

Owl turned his magnified gaze upon her, seeming horrified by the question. He tapped a rust-colored paw on the screen by **MissMonster**'s name. "False advertising," he said in his high-pitched, cartoony voice.

His answer caught her off guard, making her laugh. She'd forgotten that this monster could speak English. Snatching up the mouse, Owl continued surfing the Net.

Rilla counted the monsters. Eleven. Who was missing? Then she remembered the shy one. Leaving the desk, she knelt next to the bed and peeked beneath. Two scared eyes gazed out at her.

"I knew you'd be here," Rilla cooed to Butterscotch, the August monster. "Stay put. I'll bet you're safest right where you are."

Butter didn't argue. She preferred life down under.

Rilla stood, taking it all in. This was more exciting than Disneyland. She had her own amusement park right here in the attic!

Catching Joshua's eye, she exclaimed, "Can you believe this?"

"No." He dove to catch the ball, sliding across the bed and slamming into Sweetie Pie, who'd climbed up on the quilt to play with Rilla's pink stuffed lion.

Sweetie Pie began to wail. Rilla rushed to scoop her up and comfort her, holding her like a baby.

"This is a fairy tale," Joshua said, picking himself up off the bed and straightening the quilt. "Like, once upon a time, twelve mini-monsters came to stay."

Rilla laughed. "And they lived happily ever attic."

Whooooosh! Ker-plop!

Plop! Plop! Plop!

That was Summer, the graceful June monster-bird, landing on Bow's pile of gifts and tumbling them all to the floor. Bow sprang to her skinny legs and lit into Summer with a good monster bawling out.

Then Burly and Sparkler got into a fight over the skateboard. Icicle started grumping at Goblin, who liked to sit beneath the rocker—which prevented Icicle from rocking.

Rilla covered her hands with her ears. "Maybe happily ever attic is too much to hope for. What now?"

Clank, clank, clank!

"Uh-oh. I'm needed downstairs." Rilla panicked. "I can't leave the monsters here like this. I—I don't know what they might do to each other."

Thump, thump!

The door! Ohmigosh. Rilla stared at Joshua. "I might be able to hide one or two monsters, but not all twelve!"

Joshua stood like a statue, holding Burly's mini-football high, ready to toss. His face reflected Rilla's panic. "What are we going to do?"

"Open the door!" shouted an angry voice.

Mother Lazuli!

"I'll stall her," Joshua rasped. "You stay here and make them quiet down. I'll go out and . . . and get rid of her. Somehow."

"Oh, thank you, thank you."

Rilla ran to the door. "Get real close so you can slip out as soon as I open it."

Joshua started to obey. But before he could take a step, the battle over the skateboard culminated with one mighty tug. The board flew out of Sparkler's paws and sailed across the room, smacking Joshua on the side of the head.

He crumpled to the floor, out cold.

"Joshua!" Rilla raced to his side. "Wake up! Oh, please wake up!"

Bang, bang, bang!

"Rilla!"

That was Sparrow's angry shout.

"Oh, no!" Rilla began to hyperventilate.

"What's going on in there?" Sparrow hollered. "Open the door this instant!"

Frantic, Rilla's gaze darted wildly around the room.

The monsters were having a complete and total free-for-all.

Joshua was dazed.

And she had clearly run out of excuses.

Hysteria took her breath away. Could it get any worse than this?

✩ 29 ✩

Magic in the Skies

"Come *on*, Joshua, you promised to help."

He answered with a bewildered gaze as he tried to sit up.

Then it hit her. Joshua *was* helping.

Pulling him to his feet, she grasped his arm and led him to the door.

"Rilla Harmony Earth!" shouted Sparrow.

"One, two, three," Rilla counted. Opening the door, she stumbled into the stairwell, forcing Sparrow and Mother Lazuli down the steps as she urged Joshua from the attic, then yanked the door shut behind them.

Joshua put a hand to his head and moaned.

Rilla wasn't sure if he was still stunned—or merely acting. Either way, it was working.

"What happened?" cried Sparrow.

"He . . . he bumped his head. Badly. Please help him," Rilla pleaded, staring fervently at Mother Lazuli. "I know you can help him."

"It's too dark up here to see," Mother griped in a voice loaded with suspicion. "Let's get him downstairs."

Rilla followed as far as the second floor, falling behind on purpose. When they were out of sight, she raced back to the attic.

Of course she was concerned about Joshua, but how could she leave twelve monsters rioting in the attic? She knew Joshua would be okay under the expert care of the two house healers.

"Thanks for helping me," she whispered to her one true love as she burst into her room. The monsters were clambering for a spot at one of the windows. Some stood on chairs, some on bookshelves. Even grumpy Icicle balanced on the arm of the rocker, captivated by a sight outside the window.

What were they gaping at?

Rilla rushed to look, almost tripping over Butterscotch creeping from beneath the quilt to see what all the hoopla was about.

In the bathroom, Chelsea began to shriek, as if she, too, knew something odd was happening.

Snow had stopped falling. Clouds had parted. Now the eclipse was in full view. A whole moon completely obliterated the sun. A fiery, eye-searing ring circled the dark ball.

"Don't look at it," Rilla warned her monster children.

None of them obeyed. In fact, they seemed

completely mesmerized. She watched them as they watched the phenomenon in the sky.

Why would an eclipse attract them so much?

The room was dark, but Rilla couldn't tear herself away to turn on the lamp. She was fascinated by the monsters' fascination. The expressions on their furry faces were priceless. Awe, amazement, wonder.

Icicle's tiny fangs were visible because he was . . . smiling? She'd never seen him smile before.

Burly and Sparkler were holding paws. Holding paws? A minute ago, they'd almost killed each other.

From the top of the bookcase, Summer quietly clucked, tapping her beak against the window glass as though giving everyone a running commentary about what was happening—just like Wally had been doing earlier for the home-schoolers on the veranda.

Shamrock and Goblin stood on the bed like tiny statues. Bow peered out the window from her top-of-the-dresser perch. Cranberry had crawled out of the bathroom cabinet to watch from the desk beside Owl. Sweetie Pie was trying to urge Butterscotch from her hiding place to get a better look.

Rilla was overwhelmed. Peace had befallen monster land. The creatures looked as if they were gazing adoringly upon their Mother Ship as it arrived to take them back to their homelands.

Scientists predict other oddities happening in the

skies when the comet appears at the same time as the total eclipse.

That was Mrs. Welter's voice inside Rilla's head. She'd told the home-schoolers that changes in the December sky would be a once-in-a-lifetime occurrence. The last time it'd happened was in the fifteenth century when folks chalked it up to magic.

Magic?

Maybe those fifteenth-century folks weren't so wrong after all.

If I'm not witnessing magic, then what?

Who could she ask? Everyone would think she was crazy.

"Owl!" Rilla exclaimed. Of course. He could talk. He could explain it all to her. He could solve the mystery.

She scrambled to the desk where Owl stood motionless, raised onto his back paws, next to Cranberry, hunched on his haunches. "Tell me what's going on," she urged. "I mean, I know it's a total eclipse, but why are you all staring at it? What does it mean to you?"

He didn't answer. Didn't move.

"Owl?"

Rilla touched him. He didn't flinch.

She touched Cranberry. He toppled over sideways and lay still. She whirled. Summer had stopped clucking. Chelsea had stopped shrieking.

Rilla moved down the row of observers, picking

them up one by one. "Gob, Spark, Burly, come back to me."

Three monsters were an armful. She carried them to the bed and gently arranged them on her pillow, trying to ignore the lump rising in her throat.

She collected Cran, Butter, Sweetie Pie, and Bow. Icicle she left in his rocker. Owl stayed on the desk, and Summer remained on her bookshelf perch. Shamrock she hugged for a long moment before setting him down. She'd never really gotten to know him at all.

Rilla trudged into the bathroom and rescued the stuffed mermaid floating in the tub. Drying her off, she put Chelsea back on the shelf where she'd been before.

The attic door creaked open.

Instinctively she panicked. *Why didn't I lock it?*

Relax, you've got nothing to hide.

Rilla swallowed the urge to cry. Tears would be hard to explain right now. Stepping from the bathroom, she brushed at water spots dribbled down the front of her bridesmaid gown.

Sparrow was touring the attic, taking in the disarray, stopping to frown at the pile of wrapped gifts scattered across the floor.

Rilla waited, not knowing what to say. Out of the corner of her eye, she noticed that Owl's attention had been pulled away from the computer so completely, he hadn't disconnected from the Internet.

Rilla nonchalantly signed off for him, clicking off the speaker so her mother wouldn't hear the good-bye message.

Sparrow faced her.

"What happened to Joshua? And why didn't you come downstairs to make sure he was all right?"

Before Rilla could answer, Sparrow added, "And why is your room such a mess?"

Rilla moved her mouth, but no words came out.

A glimmer of sunshine slipped from behind the moon and shot through the window directly into Sparrow's eyes.

"Oh, look," Rilla said. "The eclipse is ending."

Sparrow picked up a handful of gifts from the floor and set them on the dresser. "Rill, I have a house full of people downstairs. I don't have time to deal with whatever you are doing up here. Mother Lazuli is scaring guests away, ranting about visions of monsters. I—I don't know what's wrong with her. Plum disappeared, so I can't count . . ."

Her voice trailed off as she crossed the room and turned on the light. "Plus your father thinks you're ignoring him today. Are you?"

"Oh, no!" Rilla was appalled to think she'd hurt her father's feelings. "I—I just got caught up with the wedding, then the eclipse. And the view from the attic was much better and, um, warmer than the view from the veranda."

"Ohhhhhh, so *that's* what you and Joshua were doing up here. Watching the eclipse."

Rilla nodded eagerly. What a simple excuse. Why hadn't she thought of it? "Is he all right?"

"He's fine. I even put him to work clearing dishes and putting out clean ones. But I need more help. Would you *please* come downstairs?"

"Of course," Rilla chirped. "The eclipse is over. My homework is finished for the year." Opening the door, she motioned for her mother to go ahead.

Sparrow gave a last, bewildered glance around the attic, stopping to peek into the bathroom. "Why is the tub full?"

Rilla tsked. "Do I have to ask my mother's permission to take a bath?" She nudged Sparrow, laughing as though her teasing was really funny.

Sparrow wasn't amused. "I want this room cleaned up by tomorrow."

"Tomorrow is Christmas," Rilla answered, acting shocked.

"Okay, the next day. And I'll be up to inspect it once a week."

"Fine." Rilla closed the attic door and followed her mom downstairs.

Why had she answered "Fine"? What about the monsters?

What about the monsters? echoed inside her head, filling her with bittersweet emotions. Something strange and unique and incredibly unbelievable had happened in her attic during the eclipse.

Something magic. And she'd been there to witness it.

How could she possibly think such magic would ever happen again?

☆ 30 ☆

The Twelve Monsters of Christmas

Rilla climbed into bed with her stack of Christmas cards and settled in for her annual ritual—opening holiday mail on Christmas Eve.

What an incredible day! How could Christmas morning top it?

She glanced at the bookcase. After moving all the books off the shelves, she'd lined up the monsters in order from January to December. The twelve monsters of Christmas. The bookcase would be their permanent home—better than her pillow.

They never did fit in with her stuffed animal collection. After all, they weren't animals; they were monsters. And they weren't always stuffed.

The attic had been cleaned and straightened (to please Sparrow). The bathtub was drained and the pile of faux Christmas presents unwrapped.

Bow's gifts included Rilla's rain forest pajamas, all her pens and pencils (individually wrapped), a pic-

| 194 |

ture of her and Mr. Tamerow from last Easter, and all of the home-schooler textbooks.

The rest of the day rolled through Rilla's mind. Mother Lazuli had treated Joshua's bump with tincture of marigold to ease the bruising, then declared him fit. Rilla had told him the amazing monster news, and he'd taken it somberly, as if he, too, knew that something so significant would never happen again.

The rest of the wedding reception had been wild fun. Rilla danced almost every dance with Joshua until Sparrow made her stop and dance with Wally so he wouldn't feel left out. That meant Tina got to dance with Joshua, too.

Rilla didn't feel so angry toward Tina anymore. *Who did Joshua kiss beneath the mistletoe?*

"Me, me, me," Rilla sang, feeling smug.

She'd danced with Mr. Tamerow, her father, José, and even Elias until Aunt Poppy accused her of hogging the spotlight. So she danced with Aunt Poppy while everyone applauded.

The honeymooners planned to leave for Paris tomorrow after Christmas dinner. The following day, Mother Lazuli would depart. (Hooray!) And Plum, of course. She promised to e-mail Rilla all the way from Sri Lanka. Her screen name was **PurplePlum**. What else?

The day after Christmas, Rilla also planned to

give her father a tour of the city. Just the two of them. She couldn't wait to discuss her spring trip to Oregon with him.

The Tamerows had found a house they loved only a few miles away. Sparrow had offered to keep (and home-school) the twins while Minna and Mr. T. returned to Finland and arranged for Minna's household to be moved to America. Having Aleksis and Elias around Harmony House would be fun, Rilla thought. She got to be their part-time teacher.

Enough reminiscing and daydreaming.

Rilla ripped open the Christmas cards and read them one by one. Buried at the bottom of the pile was a letter from Global Gifts.

Yikes! It must have come in the last batch of mail Sparrow had picked up.

Rilla held the letter in both hands, feeling thrilled. Here, finally, were answers to her questions about the Monster of the Month Club. She couldn't *begin* to speculate what it might say—so she ripped open the envelope and pulled out the letter.

Dear Ms. Earth,

Thank you for requesting information about the Monster of the Month Club.

Global Gifts has no such program; therefore we cannot send "complete details" as you requested.

However, we think it's a delightful idea. We

plan to discuss it soon with our board of directors.

> Holiday wishes,
> Ms. Karalee Patterson
> President, Global Gifts, Inc.

"No such program," Rilla stammered. "But . . ." She stared at her monster family, lined up and silent. They all seemed to be watching for her reaction to the letter. She half expected Owl to snicker and cry, "Fooled ya!"

"Whoa." Rilla's hands shook with emotion. Stacking the Christmas cards on top of the dresser, she clicked off the lamp.

The full moon was setting after a rough day of blocking out the sun.

Somewhere in the night, an owl hooted. A real owl.

How could the Monster of the Month Club not exist? Who could have sent the "cozy collectibles" to her? Was this part of the magic? Had it happened before? Way back in the fifteenth century—the last time a comet and eclipse occurred at the same time?

Rilla pictured a girl exactly like herself, only living in medieval times. What if she'd stumbled across "mini-monsters in the wild," according to the legend? What if she'd hidden the monsters in a cottage in the forest? Or the tower of a king's castle?

Rilla came wide awake. The idea intrigued her. *Could the maiden have been "chosen" to care for the monsters while they were alive? Was I chosen to care for them this time around?*

Oh, Earth, you're getting carried away.

Rilla fluffed her pillow and straightened the quilt. True, it was bizarre, but it was the best explanation she could come up with at midnight on Christmas Eve.

Closing her eyes, she lay awake a long time, pondering the mystery. She had to keep reminding herself that Christmas morning was only hours away. Yet tonight something bigger than Christmas filled her thoughts.

Monsters.

A whole year of them. Bringing good fortune her way.

And now the magic had ended.

Well, maybe not.

After all, tomorrow was Christmas, and guess what happened last Christmas? Rilla received her one-year membership to the Monster of the Month Club.

Maybe something just as exciting and magical was waiting for her right now, downstairs in the parlor, beneath the Earth Christmas tree.

Stranger things had happened. . . .

The Monster Hall of Fame

January

Icicle

February

Sweetie Pie

March

Shamrock

April

Chelsea

December

Bow

Honorary Inductees

Rilla Harmony Earth

May

Burly

November

Cranberry

Joshua Banks

June

Summer

October

Goblin

September

Owl

August

Butterscotch

July

Sparkler